Careless

MICHELLE HEARD

TABLE OF CONTENTS

*A dragonfly symbolizes a change in self-awareness,
mental and emotional maturity, and in the
understanding of the deeper meaning of life.*

After all, what is life without meaning?

Chapter 1

Jax

Five years ago...

The bottle slips from my fingers, clinking as it lands on top of the small pile of empty beer bottles already gathered underneath the hammock I'm relaxing on.

"It's your turn to get beers."

Drowsily, Marcus closes his eyes. "I'll go get some in a minute."

I melt into my own hammock and sigh sleepily.

"This was the best idea you've ever had. I'm going to park my ass right here the entire weekend."

During the week, Marcus came home with five hammocks. So far, we've only put up two of them, which was an accomplishment in itself if you ask me. The three leftover hammocks are still lying in the living room.

"Do you think you'll be able to fuck while keeping your balance on this thing?" I ask, without opening my eyes.

Damn, this is the life. Me and Marcus, all the beer we want, and the sun all fucking day long.

"Don't know. You can try it out sometime and let me know. It takes ten minutes just to get my ass settled in this thing," Marcus murmurs.

Yeah, it's only a matter of seconds before he'll be fast asleep. Come to think of it, an afternoon nap isn't such a bad idea. It will give me more energy for the party we're having tonight.

I glance over at my best friend and grin. He's lying with both legs hanging off on either side of the hammock.

"Dude, you look uncomfortable," I laugh.

I'm starting to think he's asleep when he finally mumbles, "Free-Fucking-Balling. There's a nice breeze on my balls."

"Cool," I grin, and I move slowly into the same position, so I don't tip the damn hammock. When I have my legs hanging off the sides, my grin grows. "Fuck, you're right."

Marcus laughs, lazily. "The wind's blowing us, dude."

Everything is about sex when it comes to my best friend. Not like I'm one to talk. It's as if our minds permanently lives in the gutter.

We've been friends since diapers. Our moms were best friends as well. At least, they were until Mr. Reed killed Mrs. Reed. That was one fucked-up day. Marcus was only ten, and his sister, Summer, had just turned six the previous month. To this day, no one knows the reason Mr. Reed lost his shit and shot his wife, daughter, and son, before turning the gun on himself.

Fortunately, the bullet missed Marcus' heart by a ball hair. Summer and Mrs. Reed died instantly. It happened during our summer vacation, so luckily, I could stay with him every day at the hospital, until he got released into Mom's custody. He had no other family, and besides, she was his godmother.

Logan might be my twin, but after the shooting, Marcus and I became inseparable. We might have been close before he lost his family, but during his stay in the hospital, it was as if I became everything in his life.

Those first few weeks he wouldn't talk to anyone but me. Mom made him see a psychologist, but that didn't help much, either.

Marcus became detached from everyone and everything. I was the only one allowed to see behind the walls. I was the only one he didn't pretend with. I comforted his broken heart from losing his mom and sister. I held him as he cried because he didn't understand what had happened. I took the blows when he was overcome with anger at his father.

I took it all – the good, the bad, the broken – without fail.

I took it all because there's no one I love more than Marcus, and I didn't want him to carry the full weight of his fucked-up past alone.

The horror that took place in the Reed's home rocked the whole community, but after a while, things slowly returned to normal, and people stopped talking about it.

But after the shooting, Mom started to change. Where Marcus turned into himself, Mom seemed to be all over the place, as if she lost her balance in life. The friendship between her and Mrs. Reed reminded me a lot of what Marcus and I had. After Mrs. Reed died,

Mom unraveled right before our eyes. She'd gone from mother-of-the-year to fucked-up mess at breakneck speed.

At first, it was little things. She'd spent entire nights sitting outside while finishing a bottle of wine or three. She grew impatient with us, her once loving demeanor being replaced by a snapping tone and cold glare.

It got worse after our thirteenth birthday. I was the first one to go through a growth spurt. Knowing I couldn't go to Mom about the hair making its appearance on my face, I went to Mr. Hayes. He was the only father any of us had. Even though he worked his ass off, he always had time for us. Honestly, we spent more time at Carter's house than anywhere else.

Mr. Hayes was amazing. I mean, fucking amazing. He was never too busy for us. He'd go out of his way to show every single one of us how much he cared. He never missed any of our firsts. The first day of school, first games, first driving lessons – he was there for everything.

He is the only solid in our constantly changing lives and the memory of how he taught us to shave will always be one of my favorites.

It was early one morning after Mom had left for a *well-deserved* day at the spa after a night of heavy drinking. I was relieved to find that Mr. Hayes hadn't left for the office yet. After I asked him if he could show me how to shave, he took off his tailored suit jacket and proceeded to roll up the sleeves of his expensive shirt. When he had the five of us standing in front of the mirror, he placed razors and shaving gel in front of us. He made sure to remove all the blades from the razors so we could practice first.

He started with Carter, spending time with each of us, making sure we knew what to do. I was last in line, for which I was grateful because it gave me time to watch as he showed the others. I still remember Mia sitting on the side of the tub, pulling her face as she watched us.

Rhett and Mia were the first to move in with Carter and Mr. Hayes after their parents died. That was a blow to us all. Rhett and Mia had the best parents, and their sudden deaths caused Marcus to have a setback as well. It was a reminder of what he had lost, opening up his scabbed over wounds.

Mom wasn't close to Mr. and Mrs. Daniels. She didn't have any sympathy for Rhett, who she always referred to as *that friend*.

*I don't like **that friend** of yours.*

*You're spending too much time with **that friend**.*

*I don't want **that friend** here. You're all working on my last nerve.*

That only led to Logan, Rhett, and Carter spending all their time at Carter's place and avoiding our house at all costs.

I was doing my best to help Marcus deal with the nightmares, which were there every single night to haunt him.

Marcus wasn't confused and angry like he was at the age of ten. Hell no, he was bottling it all up, and I was scared what he'd do the day he exploded.

That's when the verbal abuse started. I wasn't sure why she targeted me. Maybe it's because I was the first one to show signs of becoming a man. I'm just thankful she didn't set her sights on Logan or Marcus. I never fought back out of fear she would lay into them instead.

She walked in on me while I was shaving, and the usual blank stare she gave me quickly turned to one of rage.

"You look just like him," she whispered, her voice sounding as tight as a piece of string that was about to snap.

Logan and I weren't identical twins. We had the same dirty blonde hair and brown eyes, but that was it. I was taller than him, and my features were harsher. Logan was the pretty one with the killer smile where I was abrasive and argumentative. Logan was the friendly, light-hearted brother, and me... I was the careless, cynical one.

That's another reason why Marcus and I were such a great fit. Marcus was ruthless and at times downright derisive towards others. He was the oil to my fire.

"You're the spitting image of your father."

I got used to the cold and vacant look in her eyes, but I'll never forget how her mouth pulled down that day. She looked at me with disgust.

"You think I don't see it, but I do. You and Marcus are narcissists, just like your fathers. You're poison. Your father killed me, and Robert killed Stella. It's sickening to know there will be a day you will both do the same to some poor girl."

The words didn't hurt half as much as the gleam in her eyes. I've been on the receiving end of disappointed and angry looks, plenty of times in my life, but never the '*I-wish-you-were-never-born*' glare. It felt like I stopped being her son that day.

After that, she took a swing at me every chance she got.

You're pathetic.

You're just as spineless as that good-for-nothing father of yours.

I should've gotten rid of you when he left. Now I'm stuck looking at your face every day as a reminder that he left. One day you will leave too.

It's weird how things played out after that.

I should've seen it coming, but hell, I had just discovered the magical effect a pair of tits had on my dick.

Mr. Hayes wanted to take us all to New York for the summer break. He was taking over a business there. I'll be the first to say I was worried about it. If he decided to move, it would pretty much leave me, Marcus, and Logan screwed. It would tear the group in half.

He invited Mom over for dinner so he could discuss the trip with her. After dinner, they walked to the study so they could talk privately while we went outside to swim. It was hot out already, and it was only the start of summer.

After spending some time in the pool, I needed to use the restroom. Mr. Hayes wouldn't be too happy with me if he caught me watering the garden, so I dried off and ran inside the house.

I should've stayed outside. You never hear anything good when you eavesdrop. As I walked past the study, Mom started yelling.

"How can you sit there, looking so calm as if it didn't happen? Your wife and my husband ran away together, leaving us with the kids. I've spent the best years of my life raising those boys. I'm almost forty, and I have nothing to show for my life! I'm done sitting at home, watching as my life passes me by."

I felt a weird mixture of shame and anger brewing in my chest. I was embarrassed at hearing my mother talking to Mr. Hayes like that, and I was pissed off over how selfish she was.

Then the part of my father running off with Carter's mother sunk in, making me feel sick.

I heard a chair scraping over the wooden floor, but no footsteps came towards the door, so I kept listening.

"Are you even listening to the words coming out of your mouth, Judy? You have two amazing sons. What about them?"

"I don't care. Your wife ran off with my husband. If you had kept an eye on her, it wouldn't have happened. I have my trust fund. You can keep your monthly allowance. I don't need it. I'm done wasting away in this pathetic town."

"You're really going to abandon your sons? What about the promise you made to Stella that you'd always take care of Marcus?"

"She's been dead for six years. I was a different person when I agreed to be his godmother. They're sixteen, Christopher. You can either take them, or they can take care of themselves. I'm done playing mother to those boys."

I heard Mom's high heels on the hardwood floor and ran for the restroom. Just as I slipped inside, the door to the study opened.

"I won't stop you, Judy, but make it a clean cut. Walk away right now. I'll keep the boys here tonight and take them home tomorrow to pack their stuff. I want you out of that house by the time I get there with

16

them. I won't make this harder for them than it already will be."

"I'll be gone first thing in the morning." She didn't storm off like I expected she would, but instead whispered, "You're a good man, Christopher. They'll be happy with you."

I leaned my head back against the wall as I listened to her footsteps die away.

She left without saying goodbye.

The next day Mr. Hayes took us home to pack our stuff, after having told us that Mom was okay with us spending the summer with him.

I never told anyone about the things she said to me, not even Marcus. I wasn't sad she had chosen to leave us. Actually, it made it easier for me to hate her. It made it easier to pretend around Logan.

A few weeks later, Mr. Hayes sat us down and explained that our mother wouldn't be coming home soon. She was taking some time to travel. He really did his best to gently break the news to us. Marcus and I got up and went to shoot some pool. To me, it was just another day.

Logan, on the other hand, took it hard. He looked like a zombie as he walked out of the office. Mia smiled when she saw him, took one look at his face and hugged him. I left Logan with Mia so she could comfort him.

It was during our senior year that I struggled to control my anger. I joined a gym so I could punch the shit out of a bag and lift weights until I was too tired to care.

That's when Marcus started the Screw Crew list. He made it his mission to add as many names as he could to it.

So for the last few years, Marcus has been doing his best to fuck his demons away, while I've been trying to exercise mine away.

Chapter 2

Leigh

"Seriously! You do know what it means to take a break, right?" Willow watches me with her hands on her hips, her blonde hair piled on top of her head in a messy bun.

We could've been sisters, instead of best friends. We both have blonde hair and brown eyes. Willow is a head shorter than me and has a heart-shaped face which you can't help but stop to admire. I've been told I'm pretty but being skinny and tall with an oval-shaped face, I'm not drop-dead gorgeous. Looks never bothered me, though, because I've always been a bookworm.

"I am taking a break," I mumble while keeping my eyes on my laptop's screen.

Saying I'm a bookworm might be scaling it down a bit. I'm addicted to the written word, although my passion lies with cardiac surgery. I inherited the obsession from my parents. Being the only child of two of the most admired cardiothoracic surgeons in the states, it was a given I'd follow in their footsteps.

Willow plops down next to me and leans closer so she can see what I'm reading.

"You call this taking a break?" she asks, giving me a look which clearly says our definition of the term break is vastly different.

Willow's the only person who's been a constant in my life. I have an amazing relationship with my parents, but with their busy careers and my studying, we don't get to spend a lot of time together. Willow keeps me grounded.

When I graduated school at thirteen, Willow was determined to stay friends with me even though I'm a year younger than her. During my first year at Boston, we kept contact by facetiming at least three times a week.

What I love most about Willow is that she never treats me any different just because I have a high IQ. I still think if it weren't for the fact that Willow and I were neighbors before I started at Boston, I never would've made a friend. Being privately tutored at home didn't exactly give me many opportunities to interact with other kids, and there wasn't any time to make friends once I started school. I did my best to try to break the record of becoming the youngest doctor in the US, but I missed it by two years. Now my heart is set on becoming the youngest cardiothoracic surgeon.

Dad and Mom forced me to take a six-month break before starting my six-year integrated cardiothoracic surgery residency program at USC. I'm only halfway through my forced vacation, and I'm already feeling antsy. The thought alone of starting my residency makes my heart race with excitement.

"I'm reading an article on postoperative physiotherapy. It's interesting. It's like when you read those fashion magazines you love so much."

She slowly shakes her head, giving me a look that closely resembles pity.

"Only you would think boring medical articles can compete with the latest fashion trends. You, my friend, are in desperate need of fun."

"But –" I glance from my laptop screen to her, then back to the interesting article about a survey they did in Sweden rating the effectiveness of physiotherapy after cardiac surgery. "This is fun."

21

She shakes her head again, and her facial expression clearly says my relaxation time is up.

"I'm afraid all the studying might have done permanent damage to the fun section of your brain." She narrows her eyes at me, really getting into her role as the doctor. "You, Miss Baxter, are in dire need of a party. I prescribe a full forty-eight hours of drinking and dancing."

I scrunch my nose, certainly not in the mood to go to parties the entire weekend. Before I can argue, Willow holds up her pointer finger.

"No arguing. It's of utmost importance we immediately start with the treatment, before the fun section of that genius brain of yours, shrivels and dies."

I can't help but grin at her. "You should've gone into medicine with me. You'd make a great doctor."

She pulls a face. "Hell no, I'd kill all my patients. Fashion is my passion. While we're on the topic of fashion…" Willow grabs the laptop and closes it before pulling me to my feet.

"Go shower and put on the dress I made you, and don't you dare put up your hair in that god-awful bun. It makes you look like a nun who escaped from a convent." She pulls a face as my eyes dart to the messy bun on top of her head. "I'll curl it for tonight. You're nineteen, not ninety."

"You're really going to make me go, aren't you?"

She grins, a wicked gleam in her eyes which promises no sleep in my near future.

"I only have you for another three months before you start your residency. I get a feeling I won't see you for the next six years. Hell, I'm taking full advantage of my time with you."

Willow is right. I'll be working my butt off over the next six years. I want to make a difference in this world, especially when it comes to heart transplants.

I go through the motions of showering and washing my hair. While I leave the conditioner in for a few minutes, I quickly shave. I can't wear the gorgeous dress Willow made when my legs are so hairy. After rinsing the conditioner out, I grab a towel and pat my body dry before wrapping my hair in it. When I rub lotion all over my body, I inhale deeply. I'm addicted to the sweet, rich fragrance of jasmine.

Walking back into the bedroom I share with Willow, I'm not surprised to find her waiting.

"Let's do your hair. I'll shower while you're putting on your makeup."

There's no use in arguing with her, so I take a seat at the vanity. Willow gets busy blow-drying layer by layer of my hair. As I sit and watch her hands move, I think about how lucky I am to have her as a friend.

She shares the apartment with two other girls. I've spent some time with Evie, whom I get along with. I can definitely see myself staying friends with Evie once I leave. I haven't seen much of Della, but she seems nice.

When Willow is busy massaging styling wax into my hair so it won't go frizzy, I ask, "You mentioned a party? Is Evie going as well?"

Willow wipes her hands on the towel I had around my hair while admiring her handy work.

"Yeah, she's already at Carter's place. We'll meet her there."

"Carter? He's friends with Rhett, right?" I'm still trying to remember names, never mind who fits in where in their social circle.

"Yep, you'll meet all of Rhett's friends tonight. Carter is an asshole, so just make sure you stay out of his way."

My eyebrows almost dart into my hairline. The fact that Willow thinks the guy is an asshole says a lot. She's the kindest person I know.

"Okay," I agree, although I'm curious why she doesn't like him.

"Come to think of it, just stick to my side tonight. I don't want any of the *Screw Crew* getting their hands on you."

"Why are we going then? If you don't like any of them, we can do something else."

Like, stay at home.

I can think of a couple of things I'd rather do than go to a party.

"We're going because it will be fun. Besides, it's not that I don't like them, they're just too wild for you. They're fun to hang out with, but you seriously don't want to end up in bed with one of them. Believe me when I say they will try. They have this thing going to see who can screw the most girls."

Worry lines instantly cover my forehead. "I really don't think I should go. You know I have zero experience with guys. I wouldn't know who's being nice and who's playing me even if my life depended on it."

"You'll be okay. We'll stick together, and they won't try anything with you as long as I'm by your side."

Curious to find out more, I ask, "Have any of them tried to get you into bed?"

Willow scrunches her nose. "Only Marcus has tried. Ugh, he's the worst of the group."

I don't miss the blush creeping up her neck as she quickly leaves to go shower. There's definitely a story there.

<hr>

We've been here for twenty minutes, and I'm ready to go.

I can't dance so I avoid the makeshift dance floor at all costs. The living room is packed with students, some drinking while others are already drunk, and most are in various stages of making out.

Suppressing a yawn, I decide to go outside for some fresh air. I avoid going near the pool, that's surrounded by party-goers. The last thing I want is to be thrown in the pool. It would ruin the beautiful dress Willow made me. I smile as I look down at the pale green, silky fabric. She made me a shift dress which might be a little too short for my taste, but it fits perfectly otherwise.

I spot a table with drinks and make my way over to it. I'm surprised the table isn't crowded with students. When we got here, we couldn't even get into the kitchen where the drinks were.

When I notice only sodas on the table, I understand why it's practically deserted. I pour coke in a red solo cup and watch as the tiny bubbles fizz to the top.

"You want ice?" a deep, gravelly voice says from behind me, which startles the hell out of me. I drop the cup, and it falls to the ground, causing the soda to splash all over my legs and sandals.

"Damn it," I groan as I step away from the mess at my feet. I bend to pick up the now empty cup, seeing as the contents are all over me when I hear the voice behind me again.

"And here I thought it would take some foreplay to get you wet." From the laughter in his voice, it's clear he thinks my accident is hilarious.

"You must be one of the assholes, thinking it's funny I messed all over myself," I snap, and placing the cup on the table, I turn around, getting my first look at the guy.

Shit.

I freeze like a deer in oncoming traffic as I take in the perfect specimen of everything that's male, standing in front of me.

Even though his smug smile makes my anger grow, I can't help but drink in the sight of his dreamily carved, scruffy face. Don't even get me started on his hair which is a few shades darker than mine, disheveled and sexy.

Ugh. Double shit.

"You must be one of those bitches, unable to take a joke," he says as the smile around his full mouth curves into a wicked grin, only making him hotter.

Damn it. Why does he have to be so incredibly attractive? It messes with my ability to think, and that has never happened before.

"I can take a joke," I say, clearing my throat.

"Could've fooled me."

I watch as he pours soda into a cup. He holds it out to me, one eyebrow raised. Not even thinking, I take it from him and as our fingers briefly touch, a shiver races over my body.

To make matters worse, as I'm about to take a much-needed sip, he takes hold of the hem of his shirt and drags it off his body in one smooth motion.

My mouth drops open as my eyes dart over his chest, wildly trying to drink in every inch of tanned skin and muscle.

Damn, he might have a shitty attitude, but his body sure makes up for it.

He grabs a bottle of water which he pours out over my legs and feet. My brain is screaming at me to slap the smirk right off his gorgeous face, but my traitorous body won't move a muscle.

"Sit," he says. His voice playful and raspy, making flutters erupt in my stomach.

Placing his hand on my shoulder, he pushes me lightly back, and my body, ever the traitor, goes where it's being guided. The back of my knees hit the edge of a chair, and I sit down.

I want to say something clever that will put him in his place, but my mind has clearly taken a hiatus, leaving my hormones in control of this situation.

He reaches for my left leg, and slipping the sandal from my foot, he starts to dry my leg with his shirt.

I can't stop myself from staring at his well-toned back and broad shoulders, fascinated by each muscle rippling as he moves.

When he's done with my left leg, he repeats his actions with my right leg. Only, this time his left-hand slips up until it reaches the back of my knee while he keeps drying my already dry leg.

I clear my throat to get his attention. I'm not sure if I'll ever get my voice back with all the tingles zapping upwards to my lady parts, from where he's touching me.

"There you go, all dry," he says as he stands up. He looks down at me as he throws the shirt over his shoulder. "Run along now, your mother must be worried."

"Huh?" I grunt as if my IQ dropped to a miserable zero.

"Pretty little things like you shouldn't hang out at parties. Isn't it past your bedtime?"

Finally, a flicker of my intelligence returns along with my temper. I push myself up from the chair, not that it helps as I barely reach his shoulder.

He flashes me a confident grin, his eyes dropping to my feet before slowly making their way up my body. I don't miss how they rest on my hips and breasts for a few seconds too long before they settle on my face.

I've never been so blatantly checked out in my life before, and it makes a dreaded blush creep over my cheeks.

"That's right, my eyes are up here," I say so he'll know that I know he was ogling me. "Not that it's any of your business, but I'm nineteen. I've practically been living on my own since I was thirteen. Also, I do not appreciate you calling me a pretty little thing. Women aren't things."

Feeling proud of my ability to string a few sentences together, I smile triumphantly.

"Jax, stop harassing my friend," Evie suddenly says behind me, which makes me swing around from surprise. I recognize Rhett, but I haven't met the other guy with them.

"Your friend?" Mr. Too-hot-to-have-a-personality asks. Thanks to Evie, I now know his name is Jax.

I feel him move behind me, and I hate that my body is aware of him. His arm presses against my shoulder, and my sandals appear in my line of vision.

I do my best to ignore the fact that I almost forgot them and snatch them from his hand. I drop my sandals on the floor and quickly slip them onto my feet.

"Yeah, my friend, which means she's off-limits." Evie hooks her arm through mine and pulls me closer to where Rhett's standing. "You've met Rhett, and this is Carter Hayes. They live here."

Smiling, I reach out a hand to Carter. "Leigh Baxter. It's a pleasure to meet you."

We shake hands as Willow joins us, followed by another guy who looks like he's about to kill someone.

"Sorry, I leave you alone for ten minutes, and the wolves descend."

"Wolves?" Rhett asks with a playful smile on his face.

"Yeah, wolves. Leigh's parents would kill me if any of you corrupted their daughter."

"You're carrying on as if the *pretty little thing* is fucking royalty?" Jax says from behind me, sounding a little offended. I also don't miss how he accentuated 'pretty little thing' knowing I hate the term.

"You could say that," Evie says. She looks at Carter. "Dr. Baxter, your dad's heart specialist, is her father."

Instantly, a cloud moves over Carter's face as if Evie just spat at him instead of introducing me.

"In that case, she's really off-limits," Carter bites out. He grabs my hand and starts to pull me away from the growing crowd gathering around us. "I'll take her back to the apartment. Willow, are you coming?" It doesn't sound like a question but more like an order.

More common sense seems to return to my frazzled mind, and I yank my hand free from his grip.

"What do you think you're doing?" I seethe as my anger quickly burns through my body now that my focus is no longer on Jax.

"You shouldn't be here, Leigh. Your father will kill me. I've heard him talk about his *little girl*. I'm not pissing off the man who might have his hands inside my dad's chest one of these days."

I throw my hands in the air, actually dumbfounded by how quickly the night went downhill.

"You know what," I say as I start to walk towards the side of the house, "I don't want to be here. Why the hell I'm torturing myself like this is beyond me."

I keep walking, not looking back to see if Willow is coming. I'd rather sit outside the apartment for the entire night than spend another second here.

Chapter 3

Jax

It fucking pisses me off that I keep looking up to the apartment and wondering if the pretty little thing is home.

Della's truck has been giving her problems, and with Carter already giving her shit, I offered to help her out. I glance up, and my eye catches my brother and Marcus sitting in the truck, talking shit.

"So much for helping," I say, wondering why they even came along.

"We are helping," Marcus shouts as if I'm not standing a few feet from him. "We're here for moral support."

"Fuck moral support. You could go get beers. It's fucking hot out here."

"For breakfast?" Logan raises an eyebrow at me, clearly not impressed with my request.

I just grin and get back to work. The truck's timing is fucked to hell. It sounds like it's dying when you start it. Trust a chick to fuck up a perfectly good piece of machinery.

I wipe the sweat from my forehead before checking which parts we need to buy.

Soft laughter catches my attention, and I glance up to see who it's coming from.

Fuck me.

Leigh's standing on the other side of the truck. The smile on her face takes my breath away, and again I'm struck by how beautiful she is. I thought she was fucking with me when she said she's nineteen, but Evie confirmed it. She looks nothing over seventeen, but it might be because she's so small. Not small as in short, but rather fragile looking. Beautiful is really not the right word to describe her. She's got a waiflike delicacy, and I hate the feeling of protectiveness it stirs in my chest.

She's a little too slender for my liking, but with a face like that, it's something I can overlook.

Her eyes look like melted chocolate and her hair, fuck I'd love to feel it wrapped around my fist as I silence her with an orgasm.

No scratch that. As I make her beg for an orgasm. Yeah, I'd love to see the princess beg for my cock.

"You find something funny?" I rest my hands on the side of the truck, smirking at her. It seemed to get her all riled up on Friday whenever I smirked.

"Not really... yeah, maybe." She laughs again, a light musical sound that has a direct link to my cock. She better stop smiling before I embarrass myself by going rock hard right here in public.

"Care to share?" I keep my tone bored, and it makes her smile fade a little.

She points to her face. "You have grease all over the right side of your face. Looks like the truck is kicking your ass."

The grin on my face widens as I yank my shirt off and wipe my face with it. Just like Friday night, her eyes drop to my chest. Fuck, I wonder if she's even seen a naked guy. I doubt it. She's probably one of those women who insist you switch the light off before fucking.

"See something you like, Princess?"

Her eyes dart to my face, and I wink at her as a blush colors her cheeks. I'd like to find out if her cheeks will flush the same way when she's coming apart under me.

She lifts a tray with frosted glasses. I didn't even notice she brought us something to drink.

"Yeah, I do," she says as she places the tray on the floor. "Just a pity that such a great body is being wasted on a shitty personality."

"Burn!" Marcus laughs from behind me. The fucker has been watching this little dance between Leigh and me. I give him a thanks-for-having-my-back-dickhead glare, and it only makes him laugh harder.

"So being a bitch, it just comes naturally to you?"

She arches an eyebrow, clearly ready for anything I might throw at her today. For some fucked up reason, I'm not willing to admit to myself yet, I find this feisty side of her sexy as hell compared to the frazzled mess she was at the party.

"No, it's an allergic reaction I have to assholes like yourself."

"You really love that word... assholes. For a pretty little thing, you sure love to talk dirty."

She flips her hair over her shoulder and smiles sweetly. Yeah, like I'd be stupid enough to fall for that shit.

"You have a thing for the word bitches. But don't worry, I understand. We can't all have good taste in vocabulary."

I glance up to the heavens for help as Marcus starts cracking up with laughter. Logan joins in, only making things worse.

"Finally, someone who doesn't take shit from my brother."

I glare at Logan, but he ignores it and widens his smile as he reaches a hand out to her.

"I'm Logan West, the better brother."

I can't argue with that because he really is the better brother.

"Leigh Baxter. I see you got the personality and charm. Lucky for you, he got saddled with all the shitty parts."

Fuck, this woman is really pushing it. I give her a look which promises payback when she least expects it.

"Well, it was… fun, for lack of a better word. When you're done with the drinks, please bring the tray up to the apartment."

I watch her walk away, thinking it won't be much of a hardship to screw that stuck-up attitude out of her.

Chapter 4

Leigh

I hold the cold bottle of water to my neck, trying to cool down after my altercation with Jaxson. There's just something about him that gets under my skin.

I walk back to the couch and take a sip of the water as I sit down. Dragging my laptop closer, I fully intend on getting lost in the latest posts on all the medical forums I'm a member of.

When I read the same post for the fourth time, I sigh and lean my head back against the couch. *Jaxson West.* Even his name sounds hot.

Ugh.

Whatever I'm feeling right now feels nothing like the crush I had on one of my professors.

No, it's definitely not a crush. This is more like that feeling you get when you have an itchy bite under your foot, or when you sit on a piece of gum.

Jaxson is nothing but an arrogant asshole, albeit a hot as hell asshole. He's an asshole, nonetheless.

He's right. Since I've met him, I've been using the word asshole way too much.

Mindlessly, I look up the definition of the word.

Merriam-Webster: *A stupid, annoying, or detestable person.*

No, not quite the definition I'm looking for when it comes to Jaxson West. I scroll down until I find one which makes me smile.

Bingo!

Urban Dictionary: *A guy who thinks he is the shit. In his eyes, he can get ANY girl he wants. He thinks he can sleep with any girl. Not only that, he is just an ass to anyone and everyone.*

We have a winner.

Suddenly someone flops down on the couch next to me, scaring the crap out of me. My eyes dart up and seeing Jaxson, makes a stupid blush creep up my neck.

"Are you watching porn?" He grabs my laptop, and before I can try to get it back, he reads the definition out loud.

This cannot be happening right now.

I fight the urge to crawl under the couch as waves of embarrassment hit. It doesn't help that he's still shirtless. I can't keep my eyes from feasting on his muscular chest and golden skin. For a senseless moment, I wonder what it would feel like to run my hands over his chest.

He closes the laptop and places it on the coffee table before leaning back against the couch. He rests his arm behind me on the couch, and I focus hard to keep my eyes on his face.

Leaning closer, Jaxson whispers, "You've been thinking about me."

"Get over yourself," I snap, feeling my victory of earlier slipping away.

"Don't worry, Princess. You're not my type."

I don't know why hearing that upsets me, but I refuse to let it show.

"Like I care. You most probably find your *kind* at the nearest corner."

He lets out a sinister laugh which tells me I'm pushing all his buttons.

Glad to know I'm getting under his skin.

"Sweetheart, I like them to be of age and with a set of tits you can actually see without having to use a magnifying glass. I'll need GPS to find whatever you've got hidden under that shirt."

What. The. Hell?

His words hit hard, making my heart ache with the sting of not being good enough. I know I don't have perfect breasts, but for him to blatantly point it out like that makes me feel self-conscious and flawed.

Unable to be around him for a second longer, I get up and take the bottle of water back to the kitchen. I do my best to shove the negative emotions away. The last thing I want is for him to see how much his words have upset me.

I wish Willow were here. Hell, I'd be happy if any of the girls came home right now, but they're all at school. I should've locked the front door behind me.

I hear him get up and keep my back turned to him as he walks into the kitchen. He opens the fridge, and I wish I could trust myself to tell him to go to hell without crying out of pure hurt and anger.

"For a bunch of women, you have a lot of junk in here."

"Please leave." I force the words out between clenched teeth, fisting my hands to keep control of my temper. My wounded self-esteem is quickly morphing into white-hot rage.

When I feel his hand on my shoulder, I swing around, ready to slap the smirk right off his arrogant face. The look of worry is not what I expect, and it totally takes the heat out of my anger.

"You're upset?"

I can't believe the idiot has the audacity to look confused. I wonder how he would feel if I told him I'd need a magnifying glass to find his dick.

"Just leave," I bite the words out.

"Hold on. We've been doing this back-and-forth thing since we met and now you decide to get your panties in a twist?"

I take a deep breath.

Assault will not look good on your record. Breathe past the anger. Don't kill him.

"This… back and forth..." I take a deep breath, so I don't lose my voice from all the emotions swirling in my chest, "is over. You're a player and the second you can't get what you want, you insult the woman. I'm done talking to you."

He tilts his head, not breaking eye contact, as his mouth sets into a hard line. When he takes a step closer to me, I tighten my fists, ready to punch him if he tries anything. When he takes another step closer, I give him a look of warning.

"Princess," he whispers darkly.

He leans into me, and I bring my hands up to his chest with the full intention of shoving him away, but instead, my palms collide with his bare skin. Before I can yank away, he leans closer, pressing his chest hard into my hands.

"Two things..." His voice is deep and gravelly, almost sounding like a low growl. "One, you have nothing I want."

I clench my jaw so tightly, I'm afraid I'll crack a tooth.

"Two, let this be a lesson to never start something you can't finish."

I bite my bottom lip to keep the words from coming out. If I open my mouth now, I'm going to explode. Instead, I shove at his chest, which of course doesn't even budge him.

I yank my hands away from him, hoping he'll back off. When he still doesn't move, I look down and force myself to take deep breaths.

"Princess," he growls, sounding as angry as I feel.

Good, I hope he chokes on his anger. He loves to argue, and the fact that I'm keeping quiet is killing him.

When he grabs hold of my hips and lifts me to the counter, a shriek of fright escapes with a gasp.

"What the hell?" I manage to get out as my breathing speeds up. I'm not sure if it's from anger or the proximity of our bodies as he pushes his way in between my legs.

He places his hands on the counter, effectively caging my body with his. When he leans into me, I'm forced to lean back to avoid being nose to nose with him.

My heart is beating so fast I'm sure cardiac arrest is a real possibility if it beats any harder.

"On second thought, you do have something I want," he says with an undertone of infuriation which makes his voice sound deep.

"What?" I whisper, wondering what I have that could possibly be of any interest to him.

He inches forward until I can feel his breath on the corner of my mouth. It takes a lot of focus to keep absolutely still. Part of me wants to kiss him, just to shock the living hell out of him. The sane part wants to shove him away but seeing as it didn't work the first time, I doubt it will be of any use now.

When his nose touches my cheek, I close my eyes and will my heart not to fail me.

Be strong.

Keep beating.

You've got this.

Closing my eyes wasn't the best idea I've ever had, seeing as it intensifies what the feelings as he brushes his stubbly cheek against my skin. His hot breath fans over my ear, and then I feel his lips on my earlobe. Goosebumps rush over every inch of me, making my body feel alive with an unwanted need for him to touch me.

"I'll tell you once I've taken it," he whispers.

A burst of emotions erupts in my stomach, making my legs feel weak. At least I'm sitting, or I'd be sprawled on the floor at his feet.

As he pulls back, his mouth lingers over every inch of skin along my jawline.

When I feel his breath on the corner of my mouth, he growls, "Open your eyes, Leigh."

It's the first time he's called me by my given name, and that alone makes my eyes pop open. I'm shocked when I see desire as clear as daylight shining from his eyes.

The corner of his mouth twitches into a smirk, and it makes me worry what he sees on my face.

I don't get to find out as the sound of the front door opening makes Jaxson take a step back. I take advantage of the interruption and push him as hard as I can so he'll move faster. Luckily he does, and it gives me enough space to slip from the counter. I move out of his reach then dart for the front door. When I see Evie, relief washes over me.

Evie's eyes dart from me to Jaxson, before her gaze settles back on my face. A suspicious frown settles on her forehead.

"Everything okay here?" she asks me, but Jaxson throws his arm around me, pulling me tightly to his side.

"Sure. I was just returning the tray and glasses. Leigh was kind enough to bring us something to drink while I was looking at Della's truck."

"Thanks for fixing her truck," Evie says, all the suspicion easing from her face as she smiles. "Are you heading out?"

"Yeah, I have a class this afternoon. Are you coming over later?"

I shake my head which only makes him hold me tighter, squashing my cheek to his chest. His scent wafts up my nose, a mixture of his sweat and something earthy. I hate that I love the smell.

"I'm not sure about Willow and Leigh, but I'll come over around seven."

"See you then," Jaxson says.

He waits until Evie walks deeper into the apartment before he turns his body into mine, bringing us chest to chest. He takes hold of my chin which I yank free.

"Stop touching me," I hiss as I try to wiggle free of his hold.

"Why? Your body seems to like it," he whispers.

When his knuckle brushes along the side of my breast, I lose the little control I had left. I bring my knee up and unfortunately it connects with his thigh. The shock on his face is totally worth whatever he'll do to retaliate.

"I. Said. Don't. Touch. Me," I grind the words out.

The look of shock is quickly replaced by a calculating look. It sends shivers racing down my spine, and I'm not sure if it's from worry or anticipation of what might happen the next time we're alone.

I'll just have to make sure I'm never alone with him because he's right – my mind might hate him, but my traitorous body is very much interested in him.

It's just an animalistic reaction. He's attractive, and my body is obviously reacting to that.

He winks at me as he starts to walk to the door. Before he pulls it closed behind him, he says, "I really hope you don't come over with the others tonight. This back-and-forth dance was tiring enough for today. Oh, wait, there was no back-and-forth. Seems I found a way to silence that pretty little mouth of yours."

He blows me a kiss then closes the door behind him, leaving me stewing in frustration and rage.

Chapter 5

Jax

I'm a little disappointed when Evie and Willow come over without Leigh. I know I told her she's not welcome, but I was hoping she'd come, anyway.

"Where's Leigh?" I ask.

Normally I wouldn't give a damn whether a girl shows up or not, but with Leigh, I can't help myself. From the moment I laid eyes on her, she's all I've been thinking about.

After all the shit that went down with Mom, I've avoided feelings at all cost. I don't date, and I sure as hell have no interest in getting to know a woman.

I've never kissed a woman. Well, not on the mouth. I've kissed plenty of other body parts though. It's just too personal. Kissing leads to feeling.

Until Leigh.

Never before have I had such a strong urge to kiss a girl. When I had her up on that counter, it was all I

51

could think about. Seeing the anger mixing with lust in her eyes was one hell of a turn-on.

Arguing is like foreplay to me, and the fact that she refused to fight back, got to me.

"She has a headache," Willow says.

I stare at her, not sure what we're talking about.

"You asked where Leigh is," Willow states as she tries to read my face.

"Oh yeah," I say, hating that I'm so deep in thought about Leigh I can't even follow a simple conversation.

"She just started wearing contact lenses, and they're giving her a headache. She tries once a year but always goes back to wearing glasses."

Fuck, now I'm picturing Leigh with glasses. The last thing I need is to get wood while hanging with everyone.

"What's the story with her?"

Carter's eyes dart to me, but I ignore him. I don't tell him how to handle Della who's clearly gotten under his skin.

"She's taking a break before she begins her residency at USC. If it were up to her, she would've started already, but her parents forced her to take a vacation."

"She's only nineteen, and she's starting her residency. How did she manage that?" Carter asks.

Willow smiles proudly. "She's brilliant. Depending on which test you go with, her IQ is between one hundred and seventy and two hundred and five. She graduated school at thirteen and finished med school a few months ago."

That's just my fucking luck. The first girl I fall for, and she's a fucking genius.

I stare at Willow in shock. I don't know where to begin to process the piece of information.

"As proud as I am, I also worry about her." Willow makes eye contact with me when she continues, "She hasn't had a normal upbringing. She was tutored at home. No proms. No dates. That's an important part of growing up she missed out on."

"Yeah, it couldn't have been easy for her," Logan says.

"I'm not surprised. Both of her parents are cardiothoracic surgeons," Carter adds his thoughts to the conversation.

"Speaking of hearts," Evie says, "How's your dad doing, Carter?"

"Fucking stubborn," Carter snaps. "He's busy closing a deal and keeps postponing the surgery. I can't wait to be done with school so I can join him in New York. I'm hoping to take over so he can take care of his health."

When they start to talk about our upcoming exams, my mind wanders back to a certain feisty genius. She's a plethora of everything I want in a woman. If I were a different man, the settling down kind, I'd do everything in my power to make her mine.

Needing a beer, I get up. "Anyone else wants a beer?"

"Yeah," Marcus says. As soon as I walk away, he sits down on the space I vacated next to Willow.

When I walk by the entrance, I spot Willow and Evie's bags. Glancing over my shoulder to make sure they're both occupied, I take Willow's phone from her bag. Finding Leigh's number, I program it into my own phone. I decide to skip the beer and head up to my room. As I fall down on my bed, I type out a message to Leigh.

Me: What's up, Doc?

Like an idiot, I stare at the phone until she finally reads it.

Leigh: Who's this?

Me: Guess.

Me: PS. I'll have to up my game to match that IQ of yours.

I watch her type for quite a while before a message comes through, which makes me think she deleted it quite a few times.

Leigh: It's late, Jaxson. Can we continue this tomorrow?

Remembering she has a headache, I decide to take it easy on her tonight.

Me: How's your head? Willow said you have a headache.

Leigh: It's okay.

Leigh: Thanks for asking.

Me: So you wear glasses. Send me a pic.

I expect her to tell me to go to hell, but instead, she surprises me. A picture loads onto my phone. It's a recent photo of her and an older couple. They must be her parents. My eyes zoom in on her smile before moving onto the glasses.

Damn, she looks hot. Librarian-fantasy-kind-of-hot.

Leigh: The man on my right is my father. He'll remove your heart, as in literally ripping it from your chest, if you try to intimidate me again. The woman on my left is my mother. She's really good with a scalpel, so unless you want your testicles in a jar, you'll pay attention to the abovementioned warning.

I'm quite attached to my testicles and have no doubt her parents are protective of her, but it still doesn't make me back down.

Me: Thanks for the head's up, Doc. BTW that's a really good photo of you. You look hot with glasses.

She reads the message but doesn't reply for a few minutes.

Leigh: Thank you. Why are you nice to me, Jaxson?

Me: You're not feeling well. When you feel better, I'll return to my usual asshole self.

Leigh: Why?

Me: Why what?

Leigh: Why do you argue with me?

I stare at the screen, wondering if I should be honest with her because I'd actually be pissed if I caught a guy being a dick to Leigh.

Me: It's safer if you hate me.

Leigh: ???

Me: I'm not dating material.

Leigh: I never gave you any indication I want to date you.

Me: And that, Doc, is why you're safe and sound in your bed right now, and not moaning as I sink my cock deep inside your pussy.

Me: Come to think of it, we could hate-fuck and get rid of the tension.

Leigh: Seriously? That's never happening. You should try being decent, Jaxson. You might get laid more.

Me: Don't knock it until you've tried it.

Me: So you're open to the idea of sex with me. That's good to know.

Leigh: That's not what I said!!!!

Me: If I behave, will you let me touch you? Will you moan when I slip my hand between your legs? Will you grind down on me as I finger you?

Fuck, now I'm hard just picturing it.

Leigh: You're disgusting. Bye.

I chuckle when she doesn't go offline.

Me: I bet you taste as sweet as you smell.

Leigh: You'll never find out. There's no way I'm letting you kiss me.

Me: Who said anything about kissing? I can already feel your thighs hugging my head as I devour your clit.

Leigh: You've succeeded, Jaxson. I believe you. You're definitely not dating material. I won't be swooning over you in this lifetime.

Me: Great, so you're good with hate-fucking?

Leigh: The day I have sex with a man, it will be because I actually like him.

Me: That's where you're wrong, Princess. Hate-fucking is so much better. There's no need to worry about feelings getting hurt. We both get off and go our happy ways.

Leigh: $P' = P \left(1 + r/n\right)^{nt}$

What the fuck? I don't know if it's a turn-on or if I'm irritated that she's trying to beat me with her intelligence.

Me: I'll bite. Enlighten me, Doc.

Leigh: P is the original principal sum (You). P' is the new principal sum (Me). r is the chances of us ever getting naked together. n is the compounding

frequency at which you infuriate me. *t* is the overall length of time it's taken for you to ensure we'll never be friends. The answer resulting in me blocking your number.

Before I can reply, she blocks me. I drop the phone to the bed and start to laugh. Fuck she's hot when she gets angry which only makes me more determined.

I close my eyes, and it doesn't take much of my imagination to picture her naked. I'm not a breast guy, but I bet her breasts will fit perfectly in my mouth. I want to bend her over the bed so I can watch as her ass turns red from my body slamming against hers as my cock sinks deep into her pussy.

"Fuck," I groan as an uncontrollable need makes me hard as hell.

I shove my shorts down and fist my cock. There's already pre-cum gathering on the head, and it won't take long for me to explode.

I picture her flushed cheeks and her ass grinding back against me as she comes on my cock. Her wearing the glasses and looking at me from over her shoulder as I ride her ass.

Fuck. Fuck. *Fuck.*

My cock jerks in my fist and hot cum shoots over my abdomen as a powerful orgasm surges through my body.

When the last of the high trickles away, I still have a clear image of her in my head. I take a quick shower before getting back into bed.

Just before I drift off to sleep, a strange emotion swells inside my chest.

I like Leigh Baxter.

Chapter 6

Leigh

I sip my coffee while staring blankly at the counter where Jaxson had me cornered yesterday.

I should be upset with him for the things he said, but instead, I can't stop thinking about it. I've never had such a strong physical reaction to a man. I keep picturing his mouth and hands on me, which has my body burning with a need only he can take care of.

It's not like I'm waiting for Mr. Right to come along. Maybe...

The only reason I'm still a virgin is that I've been working hard. There was no time to date, or even for a one night stand.

But... there's time now.

I sigh, wishing I could figure out Jaxson the same way I'd figure out an equation.

While Willow's at classes, I spend the morning researching transplantation assist devices and robotic surgery.

For lunch, I warm up some leftover pizza. After I finish eating, I decide to take a bath. I'm glad the headache is gone. That's the last time I try to wear contacts.

I pour myself a bubble bath, and when I sink down into the water, I let out a relaxing sigh. I lean my head back against the tiled wall and close my eyes, allowing the jasmine aroma to chase away the last of the tension.

Once my skin shrivels up like a prune, I let the water drain out and dry myself. I take my time rubbing lotion over my body and get dressed in a pair of shorts and a t-shirt. I skip the bra seeing as I'm not going anywhere.

Evie gets home first, and honestly, I'm just happy I'm not alone anymore.

"How was your day?" I ask as I sit down on the couch.

Evie plops down beside me. "Exhausting. I don't know how you can study all day long."

"It's different for me."

"Don't you want to write my exams for me?" She makes a cute face which has me laughing. "I'll pay you with massages."

I let out a burst of laughter. "Wouldn't that be awesome? It would be a win for both of us. I get to keep busy, and you can relax."

"If only dreams would come true," she says, giving me a warm smile.

"I'm thinking of going home. Maybe I can convince my parents to let me sit in on surgeries as an observer."

"You don't have an off switch, do you?"

I smile at her. "No. I'm bored out of my mind. I need to keep busy."

Evie gets up. "I'm going to shower. Oh, I almost forgot to tell you. Willow said she's going out with Marcus so she'll be late tonight. Her battery died so she couldn't message you. I'm going to meet Rhett, Carter, and Logan for a drink if you want to join us."

With my luck, Jaxson will be there.

"No thanks, I'll watch a movie until Willow gets back."

"You have my number if you change your mind."

"Thanks, Evie."

I grab the remote for the TV and channel surf until Evie comes out of her room. She's dressed in a tight shirt and flowing skirt which reaches all the way to her sandals.

"You look pretty."

"Thanks. You sure you don't want to come?" she asks again.

"I'm sure." I stretch out on the couch, making myself comfortable. "Have fun."

I flick through the channels until a documentary about unexplained deaths catches my attention.

I must have dozed off because I'm woken by my phone vibrating on the coffee table as the shrill ringtone echoes through the apartment.

I press the phone to my ear as I push strands of hair away from my face. I glance around the living room to see if there's anything lying around that I can use to tie my hair.

"Hello." Sounding groggy, I clear my throat.

"Leigh, it's Dad."

"Hey, Dad. I was going to call you tomorrow."

I rub my eyes and suppress a yawn. Who knew doing nothing all day long could be so tiring.

"You have to come home, sweetheart."

Relief washes over me. Thank God for answered prayers. Now I just have to convince them to allow me to sit in on their surgeries. They shouldn't have a problem with it, seeing as I'll be in the gallery.

"That's why I was going to call. I'm bored out of my mind. Do you think I can sit in on your surgeries as an observer? I promise I won't get in the way."

A shuddering breath from Dad fills my ears. He must've had a long day.

"Dad? Is everything okay?"

"Sweetheart… it's your mom. She had an accident."

I dart up from the couch as my hand flies to my mouth in shock. Worry for Mom pours through my body and settles like a rock in the pit of my stomach.

"Is she okay? What kind of accident? How bad are her injuries? Was she taken to a hospital?" I look at the time and see that it's already past nine pm. "I can try to get a flight out tonight."

"Leigh, I want you to listen to me. I'll book a flight for you first thing in the morning. Stay with Willow until I collect you from the apartment."

"I don't mind coming home tonight. I want to be there for Mom."

"She didn't make it, sweetheart," he rasps as his breaths falter.

I frown, and the words don't sink in. For the first time in my life, I can't get my mind to understand what he's trying to say.

"What do you mean? She didn't make it to the hospital yet? Are they still en route?"

As the seconds slowly creep by, icy fingers claw their way into my chest and grip my heart. My worry morphs into panic and fear when Dad takes too long to respond.

"Leigh, she didn't…" His words trail away as a sob bursts from him.

I close my eyes as a cold sensation spreads over my body until it feels as if my whole body has been submerged in ice. Pins and needles creep over my skull as the realization slams into my gut.

"Say it, Dad," I croak. My throat closes up, and I gasp like a fish as I try to force air into my lungs. "You have to say it. You told me it's the first thing they taught you. You have to say the words."

A grief-stricken sound fills my ear, and it robs me of the precious air in my lungs. My chest tightens as if my ribs are trying to form a cocoon of safety around my heart, to protect it from the fateful blow that's coming.

"Your mom's dead, Leigh," he brokenly forces the words out.

I close my eyes as I listen to Dad's anguished cries.

My eyes remain dry as the inevitability of what Dad just told me engulfs my mind. The shock is still too fresh. It hasn't hit me fully yet.

Shock and denial. Pain and guilt. Anger and bargaining. Depression. Acceptance.

I repeat the stages of grief over and over.

My mind stops at shock. Shock hits first before denial strikes. *Shock*. My mind races to retrieve everything I know about shock.

Inability to move.

I blink and place my free hand over my stomach.

General pains.

My stomach is aching. It's a weird sensation and one I haven't felt before. It feels like I've swallowed burning logs.

I keep working through the facts as I try to keep my mind focused on substantiated data.

Feelings of heaviness.

That explains why I can't make my body move faster. It feels as if time is suspended while I'm touching a live wire.

Dad clears his throat. "Please stay with Willow. I don't want you traveling tonight, not while you're in shock. I'll fly to North Carolina and meet you at the apartment. I'll bring you home, sweetheart. Can you do that for me? Can you wait until morning?"

"I'll wait, Daddy," I whisper, knowing it's what he needs to hear. "I'll wait here for you."

"I'm sorry, sweetheart. I wish I could come through right now. I need to…"

"I understand, Daddy. You need to process your own shock. I'll see you tomorrow. I'll be okay." I look around the empty apartment as I lie, "Willow is here with me. I'm not alone."

After we've said goodbye, I dial Willow's number. I need her to come home.

When it goes straight to her answering machine, I end the call.

I close my eyes as a devastating wave of hopeless anguish hits me.

I need to scream or cry. I need to let the acute agony and shock out, but I don't know how.

I start to pace while shoving my hands into my hair. *Keep moving.*

"Myocarditis," I whisper as I start to recite facts. "Inflammatory disease… "

I grab fistfuls of my hair as a scream builds in my throat, but no sound comes out, only a gasp of air.

"Process it," I whimper. "Understand what has happened."

Birth and death is the natural order of life.

Death.

Dead.

My mother is dead.

"Oh, God." I start to gasp for air as my stomach drops, leaving my heart to free-fall until it shatters at my feet.

I need Willow. Evie said she's with Marcus. She must be at the guys' house. If she isn't, then maybe one of the guys can call Marcus and ask him to bring her home for me.

I run from the apartment as I dial her number again, praying she'll answer. I keep reaching her voicemail, and I only stop trying when I get to the house.

Chapter 7

Jax

I know Logan talks to Mom. Just because I don't want anything to do with her, I don't expect him to not have contact with her. I hate that she asks him to pass messages on to me.

As he ends the call, I know what's coming.

"Mom sends her love. She says she misses you."

My eyes snap to Logan. "Do you actually believe that shit?"

Logan shoves his phone into the back pocket of his jeans, avoiding eye contact with me.

"I think she cares," he says.

"Look at me and then repeat the lie," I grind the words out.

His eyes meet mine, and I hate that they're filled with sadness.

"I really believe she cares. She'll come back."

I bite my bottom lip so I don't say anything else that will upset Logan. It's not his fault. He doesn't know her the way I do.

"Are you going out?" I ask, changing the subject.

"Yeah, I'm already late. I'm meeting Rhett and Carter for a drink. You want to come?"

"Nah, I'm just going to hang at home."

Opening the front door, Logan glances at me from over his shoulder.

"I love you, Jaxson. Not because you're my brother, but because you always look out for me. I know what Mom did. I know you protected Marcus and me. You have a right to hate her, and I'm sorry that I can't."

The bitch doesn't deserve Logan's love.

"I love you, Logan. Don't worry about the shit. What she did is between her and me."

He gives me a chin lift and shuts the door behind him.

The moment I hear his car pull out of the driveway, I throw the bottle of beer I've been nursing. It crashes against the wall, and I watch the liquid trickle down the white paint.

"I fucking hate you, Judy West," I growl.

I'm glad I'm alone at home as wave after wave of anger, wash over me. I drop to the floor and start to do sit-ups. Exercising is the only way I can calm down.

I'm busy with push-ups when someone bangs on the door.

"I'm coming," I shout as the incessant hammering continues. Yanking the door open, I snap, "You don't have to fucking break it."

"Willow," Leigh forces the word out as if her throat is closing up, which immediately grabs my attention.

Her face is ghostly pale, and she's shivering as if she's freezing, while it's hot as hell tonight. I glance at the rest of her body to see if she's hurt anywhere, and that's when I notice she's barefoot.

"Willow," she croaks.

"She's not here," I say.

I reach out to her and taking hold of her arm, I pull her inside. I shut the door and take hold of her shoulders so I can make sure she's okay. She's trembling under my hands which makes worry fuse with the anger still burning in my chest.

"What happened?" I'm not even going to ask if she's okay. It's pretty clear she's upset.

I force my own rampant emotions aside so I can focus on her.

Leigh looks dazed as she stares impassively at my chest.

"Uhm… Marcus," she whispers. "Can you call Marcus and ask him to bring her home?"

"Sure," I say.

She shakes her head, and a devastating look crosses her features.

"Leigh," I whisper, leaning in as I try to catch her eyes. "What happened? Is it something I can help with?"

She shakes her head again and turns away from me. When she reaches for the door, I move fast and grab hold of her hand.

"Where are you going?"

"The apartment. I'll wait there for Willow."

I hate the hollow sound in her voice. There's no way I'm letting her walk back to the apartment with the state she's in.

Wanting her nowhere near the front door, I pull her into the living room. Living my hands to her face, I frame her cheeks and force her to look at me.

"Tell me what's wrong."

Her breathing hitches and she grabs hold of my wrists.

"She had an accident," she groans, and it sounds so painful, I can actually feel it in my gut.

"Who?" I ask, immediately worried about Evie and Della.

She moves slowly as if it's too much effort to even talk. She looks up at me, her eyes filled with devastation. It makes them look bruised as if someone has crushed her spirit. I move closer to her, wanting to fix whatever's wrong.

Her nails dig into my skin and her face crumbles.

"She's dead, Jaxson," she cries. The words rip through me like a hurricane.

"Who, Doc? Who's dead?"

I dread hearing her say Evie or Della's name.

"My mom." Her breathing comes in bursts as the shock hits her again. "Mom's dead," she groans, and her body convulses from the hurt tearing through her.

This is the first time since Marcus that I can actually feel someone else's pain. I felt sorry for Rhett and Mia. With Marcus, and now with Leigh, I can feel what's happening to them.

I feel the blow of the words as if someone punched me and the hopelessness of knowing there's nothing I can do to ease her pain.

My heart breaks under the heavy weight of her grief.

"Fuck, Doc," I breathe the words past the pain. "I'm so fucking sorry."

I pull her into my arms and press her face against my chest. I hold her tightly, wishing there was a way I could take this pain from her.

"Jaxson," she gasps as her hands clutch my sides. "My mom died. She's gone, and there's nothing I can do to bring her back."

I hold her tighter, pressing my lips to her hair. She must've just found out. She's bouncing between shock and the horrible reality of what happened.

"I'm sorry, Doc," I whisper. There's nothing else I can say to make this any easier for her.

For a while, her gasps of sorrow fill the air. She wraps her arms around me as another wave hits her.

"I can't cry," she whispers. "I wish I could cry. It's stuck inside of me. I feel sick."

Fuck, this is killing me.

I pull back so I can frame her face again. Not knowing what to say, I press a kiss to her forehead. A raw sob escapes her lips, which makes me kiss her cheek. I rain kisses down all over her face, trying to give her some form of comfort.

This is easily one of the worst nights of my life. The last time I felt this helpless was when Marcus was in the hospital after his father shot him.

"You were right," she breathes. "Feelings hurt." She grabs fistfuls of my shirt as a silent cry rips through her. She gasps for air, and I worry she's going to start hyperventilating.

"It hurts." She slams a fist against her chest as if she's trying to ease the pressure building inside of her.

"Jaxson," she gasps my name.

I can't fucking handle seeing her like this. I slip one arm under her knees, and the other behind her back, lifting her up against my chest. I rush up the stairs to my room, and as soon as I kick the bedroom door shut behind us, I let her legs drop to the floor as my mouth crashes against hers.

The need to ease her pain overwhelms every part of me, and for the first time, I break my rule of no kissing.

She brings her hands to my neck and standing on her toes, she tries to get closer to me. My tongue surges into her mouth, and when she kisses me back, a foreign ache spreads through my chest.

I hurt because she's hurting.

I break because she's breaking.

I'm lost because we'll never be together even though she feels like home. We'll only end up destroying each other the same way my parents did. I can't do that to her. She deserves so much more.

I start to pull back, but she moves with me.

"Don't stop. Please, Jaxson," she begs. I close my eyes as the crack in my heart deepens. "Help me."

"You're upset, Doc. Fuck, that's an understatement. You're in shock. We're both a mess right now. This will be a mistake."

She shakes her head and pleadingly looks up at me.

"Help me feel anything but this pain. I can't process it. I can't comprehend it." Panic tightens her features, and see her mind working to make sense of her loss. "There's a solution to every problem. If death is the problem, what's the solution? I can't solve the equation."

Fucking hell, I've never seen anything more heartbreaking in my life. She's trying to rationalize her way through the pain.

"Doc," I groan, pressing my forehead against hers.

I swallow the emotions as they threaten to suffocate me.

"You can't solve it. It isn't a problem. It's life."

Her breaths burst over my lips.

"What's the reason then?"

I close my eyes and give her the only answer I can. "It's to remind us we're only human." I can see my answer isn't enough so I add, "People die so others can live. Think of it, Doc. If we were immortal, where would everyone live? It's nature."

She nods, and even though the ground has just been ripped from beneath our feet, it's amazing to watch her extraordinary mind absorb the facts. She might be a genius, but at the end of the day, she's just a nineteen-year-old girl who lost her mother.

"I don't know how to process the pain."

"You can't, Doc. You need to ride the wave. It will get easier eventually. I know it fucking sucks right now, and it will suck even more tomorrow, but this time next year you'll feel better."

A desperate sound escapes her as she struggles to breathe through the finality of death.

"I can't remember the last words I said to her."

"Don't think about things like that. Not now."

I caress her jaw with my thumbs, keeping my forehead pressed against hers.

"I wish I could take your pain. I'd do anything to make this easier for you."

She presses her mouth to mine, and feeling her trembling lips, breaks my heart a little more. Tonight is changing me. I'll never be the same again.

All I know with unwavering certainty – it no longer has anything to do with me wanting her, but all about her needing me.

Chapter 8

Leigh

I can't cope with the thought that I'll never see Mom again. I'll never hear her voice again.

She won't be here to see me perform my first surgery.

She won't help me plan my wedding.

My children will never know how amazing their grandmother is... *was*.

Her heart stopped beating. It's no longer pulsing blood through her veins.

My entire life, I've been obsessed with the heart. I wanted to know everything about it. I wanted to conquer it, but instead, it conquered me.

I need a moment's relief from the pain, or it will drive me insane.

I pour all my heartache into the kiss, silently begging Jaxson to give me this moment I desperately need.

"You're hurting," he murmurs against my lips.

"Please," I beg, not caring about how I'll feel tomorrow. This moment is all that matters. Tomorrow I have to face the harrowing reality of life devoid of my mother. I have to go back to a home which will haunt me with echoes of my mother's life. I only have this one chance with Jaxson to take the edge off my harsh reality before I'm forced to face it.

When he tries to say something else, I stop his words by deepening the kiss. A deep groan rumbles up his throat finding an echo inside of me.

When he pulls away, I grab hold of the hem of my shirt and yank it over my head. I shove my shorts and panties down my legs and kick them away.

"Fuck, Doc, you're killing me," he growls.

I need him to growl. I need him to hate-fuck me. I need him to devour me so I can find relief from this intense ache and futile sense of emptiness.

I grip the hem of his shirt and relief eases the pain when he allows me to pull it off. I press my mouth to his chest, and as a wave of despair hits, I sink my teeth into his skin.

"Fuck," he hisses.

He unbuckles his belt, pulls down his zip, and shoves his jeans and boxers to the floor. I'm so far gone that I don't take in the beauty of his naked body. I know I'll regret it tomorrow, but right now I don't care.

He takes a condom from his wallet, and I know I'm supposed to feel relieved that he remembered, but I just don't care.

When he's done sheathing his cock, his fingers dig into my hips, and he lifts me against his body. The warmth from his skin chases some of the chill from my body. He wraps an arm around my waist to keep me pinned to him as he walks us to the bed.

When he lays me down on the mattress, he follows, crawling up my body until he's hovering over me. I bring my hands to his sides when he lowers himself on top of me until we're touching from head to toe.

He's hard where I'm soft. He's hot where I'm cold.

He's the opposite of me in every way, and it's exactly what I need.

"You're going to hate me tomorrow," he whispers while I see my grief reflecting in his eyes.

"Like you said, there's no need to worry about feelings getting hurt. Let me hate you so I can focus on it, instead of the despair eating away at me."

He presses a tender kiss to my lips. When he pulls back, he stares into my eyes with so much intensity it sucks me in until I fade away and there's only him.

Jaxson West – the enigma with the body of an angel and the soul of the devil.

"If that's what it takes for you to deal, then hate me, Doc. Hate me if it helps you cope."

Our mouths collide, and as his hand covers my breast, and I'm touched for the first time, I don't revel in the feel of it. Instead, I feed off the hatred I'm supposed to have for this man. I hate him because I need him more than the air I breathe.

I need him to help me stay sane.

I need him to ground me as my world spins terrifyingly out of control.

"I need you," I whisper as he nips at the skin beneath my jawline.

His hand trails over my ribs and stomach before it slips between my legs. This time feelings flutter to life in my stomach as his fingers explore me.

He leaves a trail of kisses from my neck back to my mouth. As he pushes a finger inside of me, his tongue mimics the actions, causing dizzying ripples of pleasure and relief to wash over my body.

I bring my hands to his face, and I fall in love with the scratchy feel of his five o'clock shadow against my skin.

When I feel him positioning himself at my entrance, a nagging thought hovers in the back of my mind. I shove it away with brute force, not allowing my reality to rear its ugly head.

He pushes the head of his cock into me, and the uncomfortable feeling is welcoming. It forces me to focus on what we're doing.

Jaxson breaks the kiss, and our eyes lock as he pushes another inch inside of me. He clenches his teeth as my body fights him, and my inner muscles try to push him out.

"Fuck, Doc, you're tight," he grinds the words out as if he's losing control.

His eyes hold mine as he thrusts forward, taking my virginity. A sharp pain rips through my abdomen, making tears burn behind my eyes as I gasp for air. When he pushes in deeper, I whimper as the pain increases. The physical pain is all I can focus on as tears spill from my eyes, bringing with it the relief I need to ease the pressure inside of me.

Just as I think I can't endure much more, he thrusts in all the way, and then his body stills over mine. I'm grateful he's giving me time to adjust to his size.

Everything is quiet as we stare at each other.

There's no grief.

There's no hate.

There's nothing but this indescribable moment between us.

From the moment we met, Jaxson has only given me dark scowls, and low growls filled insults.

Until now.

Now his eyes are gentle and filled with affection. He presses tender kisses against my mouth, accompanied by soothing words.

"You're extraordinary, Doc."

When a tear escapes his eye and drops onto my cheekbone, I finally break down and weep as he starts to make love to me. Our tears mingle with our kisses, and I straddle the thin line between hate and falling hopelessly in love with him.

"In another life, I could love you," I whisper.

He rests his elbows on either side of my head and lifts his upper half off me as he moves faster. Soon the pain fades, and it's replaced with pleasure. That's the exact moment I become aware of every sensation.

The feel of being skin to skin with this man is incredible. Feeling him move inside me is incomparable. Jaxson is my first.

I see wonder and sincerity in his eyes when he whispers so quietly, I would've missed the words if I weren't looking at him.

"Don't hate me forever, Doc. Meet me in another life so I can love you without you hating me."

We find our rhythm and move together as our bodies grow slick with sweat. When I feel a tightening in my abdomen, I whimper with frustration. Jaxson quickens his pace, plunging deeper and deeper inside of me.

"Let go, Doc," he grinds out.

Pulling out until only the head of his cock remains inside of me, he slams back in, rocking my body with the force. The tightening I felt a second ago unravels into a burst of light and sensations I never knew existed.

His mouth slams down on mine as if he's trying to devour the pleasure pulsing through my body. His body tightens over me, and he shudders as he finds his own release.

When he stills against me, he doesn't pull away but continues to kiss me tenderly. He brings his hands to the sides of my head and lowers his body against mine until I'm caged in by him.

This kiss feels different. It feels like a promise as if he's confessing to caring for me.

When he pulls away, and our eyes meet, I realize the kiss was a goodbye.

Chapter 9

Jax

I meant it when I asked her not to hate me forever. I hope she'll be able to forgive me one day. Fuck, I wish we had met under different circumstances.

I close my eyes as I pull out of her, hating that I can't stay buried inside of her.

As I push myself up, I mourn the loss of feeling her skin against mine. When I leave her lying on the bed, it feels as if I'm ripping my breaking heart right from my chest and leaving it in her hands.

I dispose of the condom and grabbing a washcloth, I hold it under warm water.

Leigh sits up as I walk back into the room. I press a kiss to the top of her head as I gently clean between her legs. Throwing the washcloth on the floor, I sit down on the bed. I pull her onto my lap and wrap my arms around her.

Closing my eyes, I say a silent prayer I'll be strong enough to let her go. She's not mine to keep.

Breathe, Jax.

Breathe past the pain.

You have to do this for her. She deserves better than you. You have nothing to offer an incredible person like her.

I place a finger under her chin and lift her face until our eyes meet. I try to memorize the exact shade of her irises. I try to imprint the feel of her soft skin beneath my fingers.

I press my mouth against hers and taking a deep breath, I savor the taste of her. I fill my lungs with her scent.

One breath.

Two breaths.

Three breaths.

Let go.

We stand up, and a deafening silence fills the room as we get dressed. I take her hand and link our fingers as I grab my car keys.

The drive back to the apartment is thick with loss.

The loss of her mother.

The loss of opportunities.

89

The loss of a future that might have been.

The loss of us.

When I park the car in front of the building, I whisper, "Wait here."

I get out and walking around the car, I open the door for her. I know it's a little too late to be a gentleman, but I need to show her, she's worth this kind of treatment, and not the way I've been treating her.

Anguish shadows her face as she gets out. I take hold of her hand again and walk her to her front door.

I hear laughter coming from inside, and it makes me feel relief that she won't be alone. Fuck, I wouldn't have been able to leave her otherwise.

I pull her into a hug, hating that it's the last time I'll get to hold her in my arms.

She wraps her arms around my waist, and her fingers dig into me.

"I hate you, Jaxson," she whimpers.

I can't keep the emotions locked down anymore. Tears spill over my cheeks, and I let them fall freely.

I suck in a ragged breath of air as I pull my body free from her arms. Pressing one last kiss to her forehead, it physically hurts to turn away from her. My chest aches as I fight to keep my breaking heart from being sucked into a vortex of despair.

"I hate you for making love to me," she says behind me.

Fuck. Fuck, I'm not strong enough.

The tears come faster as I rush down the stairs. When I get into the car, I slam a fist against the steering wheel and let a shout rip from my chest.

She'll never know she was my first kiss.

She's the first woman I've made love to.

Chapter 10

Leigh

After Jaxson leaves, a weird numbness settles into my bones, making my body feel heavy. I drag my feet and sluggishly open the front door.

"Hey, where have you been? I've tried calling you," Willow says.

I try to blink the daze away so I can focus on her face.

"Leigh?" Concern clouds her face as she rushes to me.

"I have to pack. My dad's coming tomorrow."

That's right. Focus on the facts.

"Dad's coming tomorrow," I repeat.

Jaxson made me feel.

"I'm going home."

Never again will I see the warmth in his eyes.

I won't get to feel his touch as it eases away the pain.

I won't get to love him. I don't get to hate him.

Instead, I'm stuck in limbo where nothing makes sense.

I must've zoned out because when I come too, I'm sitting on the couch and Willow is pressing a bottle of water to my lips.

Tears swim in her eyes as she watches me take a few sips.

"Why are you going home, Leigh? Did something happen today?"

I lick my lips, where the taste of Jaxson still lingers.

"My mom had an accident. She died." I don't sound like Leigh Baxter, the woman who just lost her mother.

I sound like Dr. Baxter, advising someone of their loved one's death.

Willow throws her arms around me and holds me tightly. Her sobs are erratic as she cries for not only my loss but her own as well.

When Willow pulls back, Evie leans in to hug me.

"I'm sorry, Leigh. I didn't know your mom, but I'm sure she was amazing. You're living proof of it."

My eyes tear up at her kind words.

Willow and Evie pack my belongings while I sit and watch them. My eyes follow their movements, but

93

my mind alternates between grieving the loss of my mother and trying to reject what I feel for Jaxson.

I watch the hand on the clock as it ticks the seconds away. Time has a weird way of warping when you're in shock. At this moment, it feels like it's dragging by, prolonging the sorrow for as long as possible. But when I think back on the night, I have no idea where all the time went.

The last twelve hours of my life can be split into five segments.

Mom's alive.

Mom's dead.

I hate Jaxson.

I love Jaxson.

I hate Jaxson.

When there's a knock on the door, Evie goes to see who it is.

She comes back with Carter following behind her.

"I'm sorry for the early visit. Jax told us what happened. I wanted to catch Leigh before she leaves."

Evie smiles sadly at him then goes to her room so we can have privacy.

Carter sits down next to me and takes my hand in his.

"Do you know what time your father will be here?" he asks. It doesn't escape my attention that he doesn't offer empty condolences.

"No."

"When I got home last night, Jaxson told me what happened. I hope you don't mind, but I arranged with my father to send our private jet, so you don't have to fly commercial back home."

I squeeze his hand because I can't summon enough strength to smile.

"Can I wait with you?" he asks.

I nod as my bottom lip starts to quiver.

Carter pulls me to his chest, and he lets me cry. I bury my face in his shirt while he makes a call to find out what flight Dad is on and arranges for a driver to collect Dad and to bring him here.

"Thank you," I whisper when he's done with the calls.

"I want you to take my number. If you or your father need anything, don't hesitate to call me."

"Why are you so nice?" I ask as I pull back so I can blow my nose.

"I'm just repaying the favor, Leigh. Your father has saved my father's life so many times. I'm in your debt for life."

"You don't owe us anything."

"My father is the only parent my friends and I have ever had. If he had died after the first, or second, or third, or even the fourth heart attack, we would've been fucked. You'll never know how thankful we are for the gift of his life. There's no doubt in my mind that without your father, mine would be dead."

A knock at the door makes Carter dart up. He opens for Dad, and I hear them whisper before they come into the living room.

My legs feel weak as I stand up.

When I see Dad, it feels like I shatter from all the tension of trying to keep it together through the night.

He wraps me in his arms, and for the first time since we spoke, I feel something familiar.

I still have a part of my home left.

I still have one parent.

I have a father, and I know he will carry me through the next few days.

"Sweetheart," he whispers as he pulls back, his eyes searching my face.

He pulls me down onto the couch and holds me tightly to his chest.

"Dr. Baxter had just finished a nineteen-hour shift. She fell asleep while driving home," he begins the routine explanation he knows I need to hear.

My whole body quivers as sobs seize my body. I needed this so much. The facts. No one understands me better than Dad.

"The car crashed into a tree. A branch entered the windscreen and ruptured her thorax. It severed her aorta."

Dad frames my face and makes me look up at him.

"Do you understand, Leigh?"

"Traumatic aortic rupture is a condition in which the aorta is severed," I repeat what he just said.

"That's right, sweetheart. There's nothing anyone could've done."

I stare at him and see the moment he realizes his mistake.

"When did she die?" I ask.

He shakes his head as tears fill his eyes.

"Leigh, nothing could be done to save her life."

"She didn't die on impact," I whisper as I pull away from Dad. "Did they clamp off the aorta?"

"They did, sweetheart," Dad whispers as his eyes beg me to stop. "She was hemorrhaging and sustained severe trauma to her lungs."

"They could've used a transplant assist device," I start to argue.

Dad frames my face and holds me still.

"Sweetheart…"

"They could've –"

"Leigh! Listen to me. I was there. You would not have been able to save her. Her body suffered irreparable damage."

I pull away from Dad and stand up, as I say, "You don't know what I'm capable of doing, Dad."

Dad gets up and places his hand on my shoulder.

"You're right. I have no idea what your mind is capable of, but I do know it was humanly impossible to repair the damage done to her body."

Dad hugs me tightly as everything inside of me rebels.

Impossible – It's just another word for failure.

"I have no doubt you'll prove me wrong one day," he whispers. He eases back and takes hold of my hand. "Let's go home, sweetheart."

I hug Evie goodbye before I turn to Willow.

"I'll take the first flight tomorrow," she promises as she hugs me.

"Thank you," I whisper.

Carter helps to carry my luggage to the car, and I'm surprised when he rides with us to the airport. When we get there, he makes sure everything is in place for our flight back home.

I press a kiss to his cheek, truly thankful for everything he's done for us.

He smiles at me, and if I'm not mistaken, there's a look of awe on his face.

"If I ever need a doctor, I pray I get you. You're going to do amazing things, Leigh. I have faith that you will perform miracles." He presses a kiss to my forehead, and whispers, "Jaxson cares about you."

Chapter 11

Jax

One year ago…

Marcus strides into my office and unbuttons his jacket before he sits.

"Where have you been? I went to your office to check if you wanted to grab something for lunch."

"I had a meeting," he says distractedly.

"I take it the meeting didn't go well?"

He gets up and walks over to the window. He stares outside instead of answering my question.

A couple of weeks ago I overheard a phone call where he was talking to a doctor. Marcus doesn't know that I know. I'm hoping he'll tell me when he's ready.

Knowing my friend is terminally ill is killing me.

I've started researching, hoping I'll find something that can help him. So far, I've had no luck, and the feeling of helplessness keeps growing with each passing day. It's hard to keep up pretenses around him.

"Have you ever watched people, Jax?"

"What?" I ask as I try to catch up after my thoughts drifted off.

"I wonder if there's a person out there who doesn't pretend."

I don't answer him because right now we're both fucking pretending nothing's wrong.

"I'm breaking things off with Willow," he whispers.

"Again? Isn't this the third time?"

I glance away from my computer and look at Marcus. The way his shoulders hang tells me he's serious.

"Why are you breaking things off? I thought you were in a good place with her."

I get up and walk over to him. Taking hold of his shoulder, I turn him so he'll face me. Willow makes him happy, and right now he needs her more than ever.

The look in his eyes scares the living shit out of me. They're glassy as if they've been drained of all life.

Fuck! Don't you dare give up, Marcus.

"I can't be with her. I have to let her go, the same way you let Leigh go. It would be stupid of me to allow things to go any further than they already have."

101

"Is this about your father?" I ask, hoping he'll open up to me. "You're breaking things off with Willow because you're scared you'll turn into him?" I shake him, hoping to get some sense into him.

Talk to me, Marcus! Let me in so I can help you carry this burden.

"We've talked about this, Marcus. We are not our parents. You will not become your father, and I won't be a fucked-up mess like my parents. We decide what to do with our lives. Don't push people away when you need them most."

Please read between the lines.

"I've decided, Jax. I'm cutting her loose."

I throw my hands up in the universal sign for I give up.

"I can't tell you what to do," I say as I turn off my computer. "But I can go with you for a beer."

I fucking need one to take off the edge.

We agree to meet at our usual bar before driving there in separate cars. Marcus gets there before me, and I'm glad to see he's managed to grab us a table.

As I sit down and loosen my tie, he says, "I've ordered the beers."

"You mentioned a meeting earlier," I say. "How did it go?"

I unbutton the top two buttons of my shirt and roll up my sleeves before I sit back and relax.

"As well as it could. We talked shit and never actually got anywhere."

A waitress places two beers on the table. I know their faces, but I can never remember their names. She pouts when I ignore her.

"Who's the lucky girl tonight?" Marcus asks as he scans the bar for potentials.

"I really don't care. As long as she bends over, I'm happy. It's been a fucking long week. I still can't believe what happened to Mia."

"Yeah, that's fucked-up. How's Logan handling it?"

"Okay... I think." I down half of the beer and signal to the bar for another round. "Rhett's not taking it well at all."

Marcus starts to peel the label from the bottle.

"I don't blame him."

He squints as if the dim lighting is hurting his eyes.

"You have a headache again?" I ask.

He's been getting them a lot lately. That's how I knew something was wrong in the first place.

"Yeah."

He takes a few sips before he continues to remove the label.

"Have you had your eyes tested?" I keep probing, hopeful that he'll stop hiding his illness and come clean with me.

"I'll go next week," he sighs. He finishes his beer, and before the next round is delivered, he gets up. "There's a brunette at your two o'clock. Have fun with her tonight. I'm going to break things off with Willow and head to bed."

My eyes find the brunette as I say, "Good luck, bro. I'll see you at the office."

I smile at her, and that's all it takes to get her to walk over to me. She slips into the seat Marcus just vacated.

"Hi, I'm Gia." Her voice is high pitched as if she's had too much caffeine.

"Jax."

The waitress places two beers on the table, and I settle the bill before I push Marcus' beer over to Gia.

"Drink the beer and go if you're not into one night stands," I say as I bring my own beer to my lips.

A seductive smile spreads over her lips as she drinks the beer. When we're done, I get up and taking her hand, I walk out of the bar.

"Your place," I say, hoping it's nearby.

"This way."

We walk two blocks when we reach her building. As we get into the elevator, she leans in to kiss me. I turn my face away while grabbing a handful of her ass.

"No kissing."

She smiles wickedly as she trails a finger down my chest.

"Rules," she purrs. "I'm good at following rules."

Yeah, and that's why you're a one night stand.

She's shorter than Leigh, and her tits must be twice as large. I'm a fucking asshole for comparing every woman I fuck to the only woman I've made love to.

The second Gia opens the front door. I wrap an arm around her waist to keep my chest pressed against her back as I kick the door closed.

Her hair reeks of smoke, and I quickly shove it over her other shoulder, so I don't have to inhale it.

I push her towards the couch and bend her over it. The short dress she's wearing pulls up, exposing her ass.

"So you're an ass man?" she asks as she grinds back against my thighs. I take a condom from my wallet and place it between my teeth, so my hands are free to unbuckle my belt. I pull the zip down and don't even bother shoving my pants down. I won't be here long enough to get naked. I pull my cock free and quickly roll on the condom.

I push her dress up until in bunches around her waist. Shoving her panties to the side, I position my cock and shove easily inside. It's disappointing how stretched she is.

I grab hold of the couch, not wanting to touch her more than I have to. Closing my eyes, I picture Leigh's face as I start to move.

My Doc.

I can still see her clearly. Her hair scattered over my pillow. Her lips parted while her breaths fan over my face. The tight grip her pussy had on my cock.

Fuck.

"Yes, baby. Fuck me harder," Gia groans, yanking me from my fantasy. "Oh yes, yes, yes," she screams as if she's coming.

Disgusted, I pull out and zip up my pants. I don't even know why I keep trying. I never come.

Well, there was that one time, but the poor woman had to suck me off until she was blue in the face.

I walk out of the apartment, not looking back. I just want to get home, take a shower, and get myself off to my memories of Leigh.

Chapter 12

Leigh

"Baxter, you're going solo today."

I almost fall off my chair as I swivel around. Dr. Magliato holds a file out to me, which I take.

"It's a valve replacement," she throws over her shoulder as she walks away.

"But I still have another six months to go."

"You're ready, Baxter."

I grin at the huge compliment and do my best to stay professional. It will be frowned upon if I jump all over Dr. Magliato with happiness.

I'm left standing at the nurses' station, holding my first solo file.

"Congrats," Sebastian sings, winking at me.

I look at him as the gravity of the moment sinks in.

"As of right now, I'm a cardiothoracic surgeon," I whisper.

"You deserve it, baby-girl," he says, getting up and hugging me.

Sebastian has become one of my best friends over the past five years. If it weren't for him, I would've been late on my first day. We got into the elevator together, and by the time we stepped out on the right floor, I knew I was going to enjoy working with him.

"Sebastian," I whisper as a tear spills over my cheek. "It means I'm the youngest cardiothoracic surgeon."

"We're celebrating tonight," he says, already picking up the phone to call Ryan. They're the most adorable married couple I've ever seen. "Hey, delicious, our girl just received her first solo op. We're celebrating tonight." He rolls his eyes which makes me chuckle. "Yes, babe, it's fine if you dress up. I have to go now." There's a pause, then he says, "I love my delicious chunk of hunk, and I can't wait to bow-chicka-wow-wow with you later."

I grip the file tighter as my eyes start to water from trying my best to keep from laughing.

When he ends the call, I wiggle my eyebrows at him. "Bow-chicka-wow-wow? Sounds like someone's getting lucky tonight."

"You know it. Now get your pretty ass down to surgery so you can prep, you don't want to be late."

I stand on my toes and press a kiss to his cheek before I walk away while opening the file so I can look at the patient's details.

"Sixty-five-year-old male. Calcific tricuspid aortic valve stenosis. Coronary vasculature with minor lesions. Peak gradient 62 mmHg, Mean 40. PA pressure: 49."

I stand to the side as they wheel a patient out of the elevator then step inside. As I examine all the information, I feel a sense of calm wash over me.

I'm going to do this on my own.

Clenching the file to my chest, I do a quick happy dance before the doors slide open.

Adrenaline rushes through my veins as I close up the patient. There were no complications. At risk of sounding vain, even I have to admit I did an amazing job.

I remove my scrubs and then go over the patient's postoperative care.

Walking out of the OR, I switch on my phone, so I can call Dad. He's going to be so proud of me.

I see a message from Carter and decide to return his call first. I've kept in touch with him after his father passed away. We suffered the same loss only months apart, and because of that, we became good friends.

"Mr. Hayes, I haven't listened to your message. I saw the missed call and thought I'd just return it."

"Leigh, I need your help," Carter gets right to the point. His voice is laced with anger.

"What can I do for you?"

"It's Marcus. I don't have all the details because the fuckers hid it from me. There's something wrong with his heart. He's in really bad shape. I need you to come and see him. Please, Leigh. It's Marcus."

I stop walking, as my mind begins to race. Carter wouldn't phone unless it was an emergency.

"I'll have to get approval for a few personal days. Carter, I have to warn you. I can't just walk into a hospital and takeover. I can talk with the doctor treating Marcus. I can advise you on what to do, but I can under no circumstances interfere."

"Get your personal days approved. I'm sending the private jet for you. If you can help Marcus, I'll have him transferred to where you are."

It will be a waste of time to rationalize with Carter right now. He's clearly upset. Once I've taken a look at Marcus' file, I'll talk to Carter.

"I'll see you soon."

It takes me two hours to arrange for personal time off. I hurry home and pack a few items before I leave for the airport. When I'm settled on the plane, I call Dad, so he'll know where I am.

Then I dial Carter's number.

"I'm on the plane. Who's treating Marcus?"

"Dr. Barnard. I don't know anything about him. I got more information for you. Did you know Marcus was shot?"

"No," I whisper, shocked to hear that. Willow never mentioned anything about Marcus being shot.

We're still close friends, but we've both been so busy we're lucky if we speak once a month.

"He was shot when he was ten. They removed the bullet but apparently, fragments were missed. He has lead poisoning. I'm not sure where the fragments are. Fuck, I wish I knew more."

112

My mind races to process all the information.

"I'll have to look at his files, scans, blood work," I take a breath and remind myself Carter has little to no medical experience. "I have a number for Dr. Bokeria. He's a leading specialist in Europe. Give it to Dr. Barnard and have him make the call. I've only done one solo surgery, Carter. Marcus has a better chance if Dr. Bokeria gets involved."

"Send me the number." I hear him walk into a quieter room. "I need you here. I trust you."

"I'll be there soon, Carter."

"Willow will bring you to the hospital."

Hours later, when I walk through the doors, a huge smile spreads across my face, and I rush forward to meet Willow.

Wrapping my arms around her, I give her a tight hug before I pull back so I can look at her. "Oh, my gosh, your hair! It's gotten so long."

"Yours is gone," she teases. "I love the short style."

"It's been too long," I say as I notice the sadness in her eyes. "How are you holding up?"

She shakes her head and glances away.

"I know you're not dating Marcus anymore, but it's understandable you're worried about him."

113

I don't know what else to say to comfort her.

"It's been a rough couple of weeks. I haven't even told you we're back together."

My eyebrow shoots into my hairline. They've been on and off more than I care to remember.

"I'll fill you in on the details on the ride to the hospital."

Once we're settled in the backseat of a town car, Willow hands me an envelope.

"This is everything I have. We've been looking for a way to save him, but so far every avenue we've followed has led us right into a brick wall."

I take the documents out and page through them. Only one page is of any use to me, and I examine it.

"This is dated almost nine months ago. Was this the first blood work done on him?"

"I think so."

"I'm a little confused," I murmur. "50µg/dL is treatable."

"The fragments are causing complications. They've been treating him for lead poisoning but..." she clears her throat to compose herself. "The fragments have embedded themselves in his heart."

I take her hand and squeeze it. The friend in me wants to hold her and assure her that everything will be fine. The doctor in me knows better.

"Do you know where in the heart?"

"No." For a second, her eyes light up with hope. "I've spoken to Dr. Barnard. He knows you're coming. He agreed to let you look at Marcus. Leigh..." she takes a deep breath.

I already know what she's going to say, so I make it easier for her.

"He's agreeing because there's nothing he can do for Marcus. I understand, Willow."

"I love him," she whimpers, and it breaks my heart to see how much she's hurting. "Please..."

I've gotten good at controlling my emotions during my residency, but right now, it's really hard to keep a calm appearance.

"I'll do my best," I whisper.

Chapter 13

Jax

Irony is when life fucks you over.

Hell is watching your best friend die a little every day, and not being able to do anything about it.

I've tried everything to find a way to save him. If only I had more time.

Movement catches my eye and thinking it's Carter, I glance at the entrance to the waiting room.

The blow of shock is so intense, I can't breathe.

Doc.

She's here.

Our eyes meet briefly, and it's another blow to my gut. It doesn't look like she recognizes me.

I've almost forgotten how beautiful she is.

Her hair's much shorter, a stylish bob which frames her face, making her look more delicate than I remember. She's dressed in a suit. The light, blue blouse she's wearing makes her skin look silky soft. And the glasses, damn, they complete the sexy-as-fuck look she has going.

The vision before me is definitely not how I remembered her.

Now that she's standing in front of me, I curse myself for walking away from her. At the time, I thought I was doing the right thing. She needed to hate someone, and I took the fall.

Instead, you hurt her while she was at her lowest, dumbass.

Hurt is an understatement. I fucking took her virginity and minutes later turned my back on her.

'I hate you for making love to me.'

I'll never forget those words. After telling her feelings hurt, I made her feel right before I turned my back on her.

I've replayed that night a million times over the past years. I thought I dealt with the guilt, but the moment she looked at me while I made love to her still haunts me.

Sometimes I think it's nothing more than wishful thinking. Other times I'd find myself praying the emotion I saw in her beautiful eyes was real, that she could love someone as fucked-up as me.

She's the only woman I've made love to, that I've kissed, and to this day I don't regret it.

I regret letting her push me away. I regret not fighting for her – for us.

It's clear the way I felt about her has not dimmed one bit.

"Where's Carter?" she asks no one in particular.

While I struggle to find my voice, Carter comes into the waiting room.

"Hey," He says, taking hold of her arm. "I spoke to Dr. Barnard. Thanks for giving me Dr. Bokeria's number. They're going to have a live conference now. I'll let you know how it goes."

When he walks out, she quickly follows. I get up and rush after them, definitely wanting to sit in on the conference.

Also, I'm not ready to let her out of my sight just yet.

"Carter," Leigh calls to him. He waits for her to catch up to him. "If Dr. Barnard allows it I'd like to sit in on the conference."

"I'm sure he will agree," Carter says, and taking her elbow, he walks her to Dr. Barnard's office.

My eyes focus on where Carter is touching her.

I know Carter loves Della. I know I have no right to Leigh. But fuck, I hate that he's touching her.

My eyes glide over her body, and I still can't believe she's here. I wasn't aware Carter had kept in contact with her.

With Marcus and Willow dating, the possibility of seeing her again has always been there, but now that she's here, I feel like I've been transported back to the past.

When we walk into Dr. Barnard's office, Carter introduces her.

The two doctors immediately start to discuss Marcus, using words I'll never understand.

Seeing Leigh work yanks me from my thoughts and throws me into a reality where she's a stranger. I don't really know her.

I have no idea what makes her smile. I don't know what she's done with her life since I last saw her.

She's a stranger.

The ninetcen-year-old girl hates me.

Hope spreads through my chest like a wildfire.

Could this be our 'another lifetime'?

As we sit around the desk and the three doctors discuss Marcus, I admit I'm way out of my league. They might as well be talking Greek.

"I haven't had a chance to look at Mr. Reed's file. Where are the fragments embedded?" Leigh asks.

Dr. Barnard hands her a file as he says, "In the left ventricle."

I catch the corner of Leigh's mouth twitching as if she's trying to suppress a smile. It makes me look closer at her facial expressions while I'm leaning forward in my chair so I don't miss anything.

There's no worry on her face. She's relaxed. She looks at the documents and holds up one of the X-rays.

"Is this the latest CSR?"

"Yes," Dr. Barnard answers.

"Dr. Baxter." I've forgotten about Dr. Bokeria. "Do you still need my assistance? I have to prep for surgery."

"My apologies, Doctor. I'll call you once I've assessed everything."

"Good. Please give my regards to your father."

Leigh rises from the chair, still looking at the X-ray.

"Dr. Barnard, would you mind if I consult with my senior?"

"Not at all."

"Which room is the patient in?"

She gathers all the papers and places them neatly back in the file.

"Room 413. Let me go with you."

I glance at Carter, wishing he would say something. He shakes his head as he rises from his chair as well, then holds me back as they walk out of the office.

"Now is not the time to ask questions. If there's one thing I've learned from my father's heart problems, it's that you never interfere when doctors are talking. Let them figure this out."

"Did you see her face? She looked calm, right?"

Carter's eyes lock on mine. "She's direct, Jax. She would've told us already if there was nothing she could do for Marcus. I trust her. She's going to save him."

I believe him. Not because he's one of my best friends, but because it's Leigh we're talking about.

I chuckle cynically as I say, "The life of the person who means the most to me lies in the palm of the girl I screwed."

"If I were you, I'd apologize before she gets her hands on his heart." Carter shakes his head. "Now you understand why I said she's off-limits."

When we walk into Marcus' room, Leigh is busy writing something in the file.

"Can you let me know as soon as the results come back for these tests?"

"Certainly," Dr. Barnard answers. "I take it you will be staying for a couple of days?"

They walk out together, and it stings that she didn't even look at me.

I'm going to have to catch her alone. I have to talk to her before she leaves. I have no idea what I'm going to say, but I can't just let her disappear out of my life again. I need to see if there's anything still between us.

Chapter 14

Leigh

Sitting in the dark, I watch as Marcus sleeps.

He's high risk. If he dies on my table, it will destroy everything I've worked hard to achieve over the past years. It will destroy my credibility.

Even if he survives the surgery, the odds he'll survive thirty days post-operation isn't good.

He wakes up and looks at me for a while before he says, "No one will blame you."

"For what?"

"Come on, Doc. We both know there's no way I'm walking out of here."

Doc.

Jaxson never called me that in front of Marcus. Does it mean they talked about me?

I stand up and slowly walk to the bed. Looking down at Marcus, I stare into his eyes until he drops the wall and lets me in.

I see despair mixed with hope, and his strength fighting against the bleakness of his situation.

"You have two options, Mr. Reed. You can give up and die in this bed, or you can ask to be transferred to my care."

A fire ignites in his eyes as he asks, "What will happen if you take me on as a patient, Dr. Baxter?"

"You will live."

There are no certainties in this life. It's something Dad has repeatedly tried to get me to believe. We're taught not to make promises to patients. We're trained to avoid using certainties where risk is involved.

"I believe in facts. I will remove the fragments, and you will not die on my table. Your psychological state plays a big part in recovery. Do you want to live, Mr. Reed, or have you already given up?"

"Of course I want to live," he growls.

"Good. I'll take a chance on you if you are willing to take a chance on me."

"Leigh," he whispers, clearly exhausted, "I'll do whatever you want me to do."

"You should be released in three days. They've stabilized you. You need to rest, Marcus. I'm going back to California. I'll arrange with Carter to bring you to California on the twenty-sixth."

I pick up my bag, and as I prepare to leave, Marcus says, "He loves you."

I take a deep breath and smile at Marcus.

"Your heart is the only one I'm interested in, Mr. Reed. Have a good night's rest."

As I step out of the elevator and walk towards the exit, I slip on my jacket. I decide to walk back to the hotel I'm staying at while calling Dad. It's freezing outside, but refreshing at the same time.

"Hi, Daddy. Did I wake you?"

"No, I was just thinking about you. How's your trip?"

"It's good. I'll talk to you about the patient when I get home." I smile as I continue, "I had my first solo today."

"You did? Sweetheart, that's wonderful. How did it go?"

"No complications."

"I'm proud of you. I wish your mother were here to see how well you've done. She would've been proud."

"Me too, Daddy." I clear my throat and force a smile to my face. "I'll be back tomorrow. Would you

125

like to come over for dinner on Friday evening so we can celebrate?"

"Of course. I'll bring wine."

"Try to get some rest. Bye, Daddy."

I drop my phone back into my bag and wrap my arms around myself to ward off the cold. As I walk into the lobby of the hotel, I see Jaxson sitting in the reception area. While he's looking at his phone, I quickly walk to the elevators. I press the button and watch as the numbers change.

Come on.

I suppress the urge to glance over my shoulder.

Please. Please. Please.

The elevator dings and I impatiently wait for a couple to exit. As I step forward, I feel a hand on my lower back.

Shit.

A quick glance over my shoulder confirms the hand belongs to Jaxson. He follows me into the elevator, and I press the number for my floor.

My eyes scan the reception area, hoping someone will come running towards the elevator, and we won't have to ride alone.

No one joins us, and the doors slide shut.

His hand moves to my hip, and then his chest presses against my back.

It's been almost six years. Jaxson belongs to a time of confusion and heartache. I didn't understand why Mom had to die. I didn't understand what happened between Jaxson and me.

I still don't.

What I do understand now is I blamed Jaxson for the pain I suffered that day. I blamed him because it was easier than admitting I felt something more than hate for him.

I don't believe in the romantic kind of love fairytales teach us about. People believe they fall in love when it's only elevated hormone levels because they like what they see.

Hate is a strong word, and it's one I've really considered when it comes to Jaxson West. I've settled for intensely disliking him. Asking me to forgive Jaxson, is like asking me to willingly sit through a root canal.

I dislike him because he had no problem taking my virginity before tossing me aside. He walked away from me when I needed someone most.

For a blinding moment, he made me believe there could be such a thing as love.

He leans into me and presses his cheek against my hair. I hear him take a deep breath, and I close my eyes.

I haven't had a chance to get a good look at him, but he still feels the same.

"Hi, Doc," he whispers. His voice is deep and rougher sounding than I remember. It still has the power to send goosebumps racing over my body.

"Jaxson," I say, glad when my voice sounds normal.

The elevator stops on my floor and the second the doors open, I dart forward. I can feel him right behind me as I walk to my room. I swipe the keycard and push open the door, walking to the bar so I can get some water.

"I'd offer you something to drink, but you won't be staying long," I say as I take a bottle of water from the fridge.

"How have you been, Doc?"

I'm angry that I'm the only one affected by this meeting. I've thought about Jaxson a lot over the past years. They say when you lose someone, their voice is the first thing you forget.

I can't remember what Mom sounded like. I can't remember her smile. Lately, I've been struggling to picture her face.

That didn't happen with Jaxson.

I turn around and face him. He's standing in the middle of the living room, and I can see every inch of him clearly under the fluorescent light.

His hair is still all over the place, and it looks hot. He's taller than I remember. The suit fits his muscled body perfectly. My eyes stop at his chest where the top two buttons of his shirt are undone. His tie hangs loosely around his neck.

There is no smirk around his mouth as my eyes travel up.

The same mouth kissed me.

Our eyes meet, and it feels as if an electric bolt strikes right through my heart.

Those eyes made me promises he had no intention of keeping.

"Let's skip the niceties and get to the point of why you're here."

He shoves one hand in his pocket, and the other goes to his chin. I hear the bristliness of his day-old stubble as he scrubs his palm over his jaw.

I don't remember him looking so serious. Suddenly I have a need to see if his smile still looks the same.

"I've just come from seeing Marcus." His hand drops to his side and worry instantly clouds his face.

I remember that look.

My breathing speeds up as memories flash through me. He had the same look when he saw me standing at his front door.

"Can you help him?" he whispers as if he's too scared to even ask, never mind hear the answer.

"Yes."

He jerks as if I slapped him, instead of giving him good news.

His breathing speeds up, and when his eyes start to shine with unshed tears, I realize he's overwhelmed. He stalks toward me, and before I can stop him, he yanks me to his chest. His arms wrap around my body, and he lifts me off my feet. I grab hold of his shoulders with the full intention of pushing him away when he presses his face into my neck, and his body shudders against mine.

When the first sob rips from his chest, I don't have it in me to push him away. Instead, I wrap my arms around his neck and cradle his head, and I give him the comfort he once gave me.

Once he gains control over his emotions, he whispers, "I'm sorry, Doc."

"It's normal to react emotionally when given good news relating to a loved one."

He pulls back but doesn't let go of me. His eyes find mine, and I try to ignore the longing I see in them.

"I'm sorry, Doc," he repeats. "I'm sorry I walked away."

I wiggle myself free from his arms and take a step away from him.

"I'll arrange with Carter to have Marcus brought to California. I'll need to run more tests, but the surgery should be scheduled for the thirtieth."

His lips curve into a smile, and it's my turn to look like I've been slapped.

There's nothing more beautiful in this world than Jaxson West smiling.

I blink the thought away and straighten my blouse to keep from looking at him.

"You haven't changed," he says. "Except for your hair. It suits you. You look beautiful, Doc."

Being direct has never let me down before.

131

"We had sex, Jaxson. That's all it was. Just sex. We were never in love." I make air quotations when I say *in love*. "We weren't even friends. I didn't like you, and you didn't like me. I'm operating on Marcus because I know I can repair the damage to his heart. I'm not doing it for you."

His smile widens, which makes me frown.

"Why are you smiling?"

"You really haven't changed at all." He closes the gap between us and presses a kiss to my forehead. Keeping his lips against my skin, he whispers, "The fact that you brought up our history tells me it meant just as much to you as it did to me. I'll be in touch."

I stand there gaping like a fish out of the water as I watch him leave.

The arrogant ba –

My thoughts screech to a halt.

Crap, wait a second...

Ugh, he's right.

"He can't be right!" I snap at myself.

You know he's right.

He asked me how I've been and gave me a compliment. He even apologized! He was nothing but well-mannered.

I cover my face with my hands as embarrassment washes over me.

The night we spent together might mean something to me, but I'm certainly not ready to examine it.

Chapter 15

Jax

When they place the tray of food on the stand, I reach over and lift off the lid. I take the dessert and lean back in the chair.

"How can you eat that shit?" Marcus asks with a look of disgust on his face.

"I take the spoon and scoop it up then shove it in my mouth," I say, grinning from ear to ear.

"Wiseass," he mumbles. "Why are you in such a good mood?"

I finish off the dessert first and lick the spoon clean before I place the empty bowl back on the tray.

"I saw Leigh last night," I say, and I'm surprised when Marcus frowns. I thought he'd be happy for me.

"Dude, can you wait until she's done slicing into my heart before you piss her off?"

"Why do you think I'm going to piss her off?"

Marcus never lies to me, so I'm not surprised when he says, "She's different, Jax. Her mind doesn't work the way ours do. You told me yourself. She doesn't care about emotions, she cares about facts. The fact is you screwed her."

"In another life, I could love you," I whisper.

Marcus looks at me as if I've lost my mind.

"It was something she said to me the night we got together."

"Sorry to break it to you, bro. That was before you dumped her ass back at the apartment."

"It's been years, Marcus. We can get to know each other. We can date. This can be our chance at that life."

"Why do you want to put yourself through that? You were a mess after she left. You live in New York, and she lives on the other side of the fucking country. You're not even in the same time zone."

He's right. We do live on opposite sides of the country.

"At most, it's a six-hour flight," I say, already planning ways to see her.

"Jax, just let it go. So she was the best you had. It doesn't mean you're fucking soulmates or some equally sappy shit. Why can't you just let her go?"

"I kissed her," I whisper. I never told him that.

"You never kiss."

I smile at him. "That's why I'm not giving up."

"I told her you love her." He shakes his head. "You know what she said?"

"She hates me? How the fuck should I know," I snap, a little pissed he told her how I feel about her.

"She said my heart is the only heart she's interested in. I believe her, Jax. She's the kind of person who lives for her job. There is no place for you in her life. She's a fucking genius. Her world is based on facts, proven fucking facts. Her kind doesn't believe in things like love, and death, and Adam and fucking Eve, Jax!"

"That's where you're wrong." I stand up and push the tray with food closer to him. "It's not that she was the best I've ever had. It's the way she looked at me. Besides you, she's the only one who's ever looked past the bullshit. Asking me to leave her..." I take a deep breath while looking at my best friend. "It's the same as asking me to leave you, Marcus. I didn't give up on you. I won't give up on her. I'll make her understand. I'll prove to her it's a fucking fact that I love her. It's a fact that she feels something for me. I have to show her feelings don't hurt."

Letting out a sigh, he whispers, "I get it. Leigh is to you what Willow is to me."

I smile at him as I finally understand why he keeps going back to Willow. She's his person.

"Eat the food. I'll check in on you after work."

He picks up the fork and stabs at the piece of chicken.

"It's fucking tasteless. It makes the metallic taste in my mouth worse."

"She's going to fix you," I whisper and suddenly a wave of emotion hits me hard.

The expression on Marcus' face jumps from hope to fear and back to hope. I place my hand on his shoulder and give it a squeeze.

"Doc won't let you die, Marcus. It's not in her to fail. If she thought there was even the slightest chance you could die, she wouldn't do it."

"You really believe that?"

Tears well in his eyes, and it makes it harder for me to control my emotions.

"It's a fact, Marcus."

"Keep it in mind when she rejects you. If she thinks there's a chance things won't work out between you, she'll push you away."

We're finally on the same page.

"Thanks, Marcus. It helped to talk things out with you. I'll see you later. Eat the shit and sleep."

When I get back to work, I go directly to Carter's office. I tap on the door before entering.

"Do you have a minute?" I ask as I sit down across from him.

"Sure. Did you just come from the hospital?" He leans back in his chair and gives me his undivided attention.

"Yeah, thanks for calling Leigh. Talking about Leigh, what time is her flight?"

"Why, Jax?"

I let out a burst of laughter. "So I can see her before she leaves."

Carter gets a serious expression on his face, which makes him look just like his father.

"I never told you I saw Leigh before she left."

Fuck. I thought only Marcus knew I slept with Leigh.

"I was there when her dad arrived at the apartment. It was… different. I can't even explain what I saw, Jax. They didn't huddle together and mourn their loss. He spoke to her as if he was telling a stranger a loved one

138

didn't make it. She didn't respond like a girl who just lost her mother."

He lets out a heavy breath and shakes his head as if what he saw still doesn't make sense to him.

"She challenged him. She wanted to know exactly when her mother died. I mean down to the last detail and her dad told her. Fuck, I'd be traumatized for life if someone had to tell me my dad died like that... but not Leigh. She needed to understand she couldn't save her mother. It was fucking heartbreaking."

I take a deep breath as regret grips my heart. I should've stayed with her. Fuck, I was stupid. I let her push me away while she needed me the most.

"I'm not telling you this to make you feel like shit. I'm telling you this, so you'll understand she's different. You're polar opposites."

I lean forward and look Carter in the eyes. "Marcus said the same thing to me. I understand you're looking out for her."

He opens his mouth to say something, but I hold up my hand.

"And you're looking out for me. What you and Marcus need to understand is I know all of those things. I love her because she's different. She challenges me.

It's because she's my opposite that we fit so perfectly together. Now please tell me what time her flight is."

"It's at three."

"Thank you."

I get up and look at the time as I leave his office. It's ten am. I have five hours to get everything ready.

Chapter 16

Leigh

When I walk into Starbucks, I take a deep breath of the aroma. Glancing around, I spot Willow where she's sitting at a table near the window. I make my way over to her and place my bag next to the table.

"Have you ordered yet?"

"Yes, and I got your favorite, so you can sit."

When I'm seated, I smile at her. Seeing her now, I feel much better than I did yesterday. Knowing I can help Marcus makes a significant difference in the atmosphere between us.

"Marcus told me you're going to operate on him."

She takes hold of my hand and gives it a squeeze. I can see the hope and gratefulness swirling in her eyes, and it's all the thanks I need.

"How are you?" I ask, just wanting to catch up with my friend.

"Work is okay. I don't get to design my own pieces yet. It's a family-owned business, so there isn't exactly room for growth, you know."

"Can't you find work at a fashion house who will allow you to make your own pieces?"

They call Willow's name, and she leaves to collect our order.

She hands me mine, and I take a deep breath of the rich aroma. "Thank you."

"I need the experience," she continues our conversation before taking a sip of her beverage. "How have you been? How's your dad?"

"He's doing well. Still stubborn as hell."

"And you?" she asks from over the rim of her cup.

"I finished my residency." A memory flashes through my mind, and I let out a chuckle. "The last time I visited you, you were right when you said we wouldn't see each other for six years. I can't believe how time has just flown by."

"At least we kept in contact," she says but takes a deep breath when her eyes well with tears. "I miss you. I didn't realize how much I needed to see you until yesterday."

"Me too. It's really good seeing you again."

142

"It was nice of Mia and Logan to get married in Marcus' room yesterday. It meant a lot to him."

"Yes. I didn't expect to be invited. I felt a little out of place, but it was beautiful to see."

I got to meet Danny, and she's just as precious as I expected her to be. I'm happy for Carter that he found Della.

It's actually weird that I've grown closer to Carter than I am with Willow. I need to reconnect with my friend.

"Are you going to come with Marcus to California?"

"I have a meeting with one of the owners today, so I can ask for time off."

"You're welcome to stay at my place."

"I'll take you up on that."

Our conversation feels stilted, and I miss the easy-going feel we always had.

"Remember when I came back into the apartment, and I told you my mom died?"

"Yeah," she whispers.

"I was with Jaxson that night."

Instantly her facial expression changes from somber to curious as she leans forward.

"With him, or *wiiith* him?" She wiggles her eyebrows to emphasize the word.

"I slept with him," I whisper as a blush creeps up my neck.

"Why didn't you tell me?" Leaning both her elbows on the table, she rests her chin on her linked fingers.

I must've pulled a face because her eyes widen.

"Was it that bad?" she gasps.

I start to laugh and shake my head. "Actually, the opposite of bad. It was amazing." I search for the right words before I continue, "You know I'm not good at expressing my feelings, but when I was with him, it felt so natural. It felt right."

"What went wrong?" she asks gently, obviously seeing on my face that it hurts to talk about it.

"He was supposed to make me hate him, but instead he made me fall in love with him," I admit the words out loud for the first time.

"I'm not following. Why was that a bad thing?"

"Because I didn't just lose my mom, Willow. I lost Jaxson as well. It multiplied the pain and grief."

It still hurts.

Shock flashes across her face, then it's quickly replaced by anger.

"He walked out on you?" she hisses. "You should've told me, Leigh."

"He walked away because I told him to," I whisper.

She scrunches her face, clearly confused.

"Love is a foreign concept for me. I mean the *romantic* kind."

"Why? It's no different from any other kind."

She has a point. I don't know how to explain myself. I look at my hands and spread them open on the table.

"I can trust my hands to do exactly what I need them to do. I know they won't tremble when I hold a scalpel. They'll make a perfect incision. They're steady and trustworthy."

"I get that you only trust what you see. You love your dad, right? You trust him?"

"I do, but he's my father, Willow. He raised me. He's protected me since I took my first breath. He's proven over and over he will never fail me."

"I get it now," she sighs as she leans back in her chair. "Your dad proved himself to you before you even knew what love was. Jaxson walked away after you realized you were in love with him."

"When I met him the night of the party… it was like striking a match. It's as if chemicals reacted, causing a combustion every time we spoke. He made me feel something I've never felt before."

She tilts her head and pins me with a serious look.

"You mentioned that earlier. You do know feeling something for someone is a good thing, right?"

I let out a burst of laughter which quickly turns sour.

"Not when it hurts, Willow. That night almost broke me. For a while, I really thought it did. I won't be able to cope with that kind of pain a second time."

Her expression turns gentle, and she smiles warmly.

"It's been almost six years. You've both changed. Jaxson is not the kind of man who walks away from those he loves."

"I know." I look down at the caramel liquid in my cup. "He's an amazing friend, just not to me. He's supportive, understanding, caring, and loving, just not to me."

"It's because you didn't get to know him, Leigh. You just met him when your mother passed away. You had a night of wild sex, which I only found out about now. I'm not happy about that." Her lips form an O as

146

she realizes something. "Hold on." With wide eyes, she stares at me. "Was Jaxson your first?"

I want to crawl under the table as my face flushes. It's funny how I have so much confidence when I walk into a hospital, but in everyday life, I have none.

"He was my only," I say so quietly, Willow has to lean in to hear me.

"Well, that explains it all."

"It does?"

I hate being confused. It makes my insides feel chaotic.

"You shared something special with him. You opened yourself up to him in a way you never have before. You were vulnerable, emotional... you were one hell of a mess," she adds dryly. "I felt the same when I had sex for the first time."

I frown at her. "You did?"

She leans forward, a look of understanding adding warmth to her gentle smile.

"You had no one to talk to. If I had known, I could've explained it to you. But I'm here now, so let me sum it up for you."

I feel a twinge of sadness that I haven't been a better friend to Willow since my mom died. Willow

147

understands the way my mind works. It's only her and Dad. Knowledge is my coping mechanism. I'm a realist. I lean forward, ready to absorb whatever information she's going throw my way.

"At some point, you and Jaxson made a connection. You liked what you saw, and he obviously liked what he saw. There was a spark. You know, like the combustion you referred to earlier."

I nod to show her I understand. It's kind of similar to the big bang effect.

There was one hell of a big bang between Jaxson and me, that's for sure.

"When you slept with him, you let him in. Not just literally. You connect with the person on a deeper level. Again, not just literally." She smiles, teasingly. "I just had to say that."

We laugh, and it eases some of the tension.

"I don't need to explain it to you, Leigh. You just have to admit to yourself you like him. I think the problem is because you fell in love with him when you lost your mom, you're scared you'll lose him as well. You don't want to take the risk of letting him in because you're scared of what may happen. You don't know if things will work out, or if they will. You don't

148

know if you'll have one year with him or fifty. It's normal to feel that way."

She looks at me, pleadingly. "I can tell you one thing, though. You'll regret it if you let him go. One year with him might be better than nothing at all. That's why I'm with Marcus. I'd rather have these last few days with him and know I was loved than walk away and wonder what it could've been like."

She's right. I've been lying to myself. I've tried so hard to convince myself that I hate him because I'm scared of how I feel when I'm around him.

"Why is it so scary to love someone?" I whisper.

"It's only scary if you focus on the probability that you can lose the person. If you focus on the present and take it one day at a time, it's not as scary. You have to decide which will hurt more – taking a chance on a man who could make you happy, or never taking a chance at all and growing old alone. Personally, living my life alone scares the living hell out of me."

"I hear what you're saying." I sigh and glance out of the window. "It's been almost six years, Willow. He's changed and so have I. Honestly, I don't think we'll get together. I just needed to talk to someone about it. You know, make sense of it all for myself."

Willow gets up, and when I do the same, she gives me a hug.

"You need to get going, or you'll miss your flight. Just remember you can talk to me about anything. We might live in different states, but I'll always be there for you."

When I pull back, I press a kiss to her cheek.

"Thank you. I really needed this." We look at each other for a little while, and then I give her the peace of mind she just gave me by saying, "I'm going to fix him."

She nods as her eyes well with tears.

"I believe in you, Leigh."

We walk out together and give each other one more hug before going our separate ways.

Chapter 17

Jax

I make sure I'm on the jet well before Leigh is due to arrive.

"Mr. West," the stewardess greets me with a clear look of surprise on her face. It doesn't stop her from checking me out. "We weren't expecting you. I'm Tia, and I'll be your stewardess for the flight." There's a flirting tone to her words which I choose to ignore.

"It was a last-minute decision." I glance around the luxurious cabin. "It's a surprise for Dr. Baxter so I'll appreciate if you don't let her know I'm onboard once she arrives. I've also brought food which I'd like to be served after we've taken off."

I keep my voice professional and hand her the brown paper bags filled with eats we can snack on and a bottle of light white wine. My plan is to get to know Leigh better and to allow her to get to know me. We need to erase the gap between us that formed over the past few years.

I take a seat in the staff area and strap myself in. My heart starts to beat with both anxiety and excitement, thinking that in a few minutes' time, I'll be sitting across from Leigh. She'll have to give me her undivided attention seeing as there's nowhere she can run to until we land.

I have around six hours to convince her to give us a try.

Once we've reached cruising altitude, I remove the seatbelt and make my way to the kitchen.

Finding Tia there, she helps me unpack and plate all the food. She tries to rub up against me every chance she gets, which irritates me to hell and back.

"Could you please prepare the table, Tia?" I ask briskly, handing her a white tablecloth and candles.

"Of course, Mr. West." Her voice is throaty as if she's willing to do just about anything I ask of her, including going down on her knees to suck me off.

I peek through the curtain and watch as Leigh stares out of the window. At least, I still have the surprise factor on my side.

She's wearing a pair of black slacks, and a white blouse which fits her frame perfectly, especially her pert breasts. The cold air makes her nipples strain against the material, and I suppress a soft groan while adjusting myself so my hard-on isn't so damn obvious.

Leigh looks comfortable, which I'm happy to see. The less tense she is when we talk, the better my chances will be when I'm pleading my case.

Once Tia is done setting everything up, I slowly pull the curtain aside. Leigh doesn't notice as I come in and I get to drink in her beauty for a little while longer. When I sit down next to her, her head turns to me and a look of surprise flashes over her face.

"I didn't know you'd be on this flight," she says, her beautiful brown eyes still wide.

"I wanted to surprise you," I admit. I don't have time to play games with her.

"Me? Why?" She turns her body, so she's facing me, and I take it as a good sign that she's not giving me the cold shoulder.

I have to choose my words carefully. I don't want to scare her away with a sudden declaration of love.

"You're someone I'd like to get to know better."

153

She frowns as if she can't understand why I'd like to get to know her. It's actually refreshing. Most of the women I've hooked up with always assume it means something more than a casual fling. And then there are the few who feel they have a right to me, and the wealth that comes with working at Indie Ink. Not one of them has ever looked at me without seeing dollar signs.

Leigh's eyes hold mine for a moment. When she looks at me like that, I know she's trying to study me, searching for the truth behind my actions.

She glances out the window again, and whispers, "I'm still the same person, Jaxson. All I do is work. I don't have time for friends."

Always direct. I don't think she has it in her to lie.

"Have a late lunch with me, Doc. When the plane lands, and you still feel the same, I promise to let it go."

Her eyes dart to me. "Just lunch?"

"Just lunch."

"Okay," she whispers.

I get up and taking her hand, I walk her over to the table. I wait until she's seated before I take the seat next to her. She glances at the empty seats across from us before looking back to me. I ignore the silent question, and with a nod in Tia's direction, I give her the sign to bring out the platter.

Tia places the platter in the middle of the table before she opens the wine. She pours some into crystal glasses before she disappears back into the kitchen, giving us privacy.

Leigh looks at the food and smiles teasingly. "What would you have done with the food if I had refused?"

"Most likely eat it all. I'm a comfort eater."

She lets out a soft chuckle. Her delicate fingers wrap around the stem of the wine glass, and she takes a small sip. Her tongue darts out, and she licks her lips. Placing the glass back on the table, her hand returns to her lap.

I decide to get the apology out of the way. We have to move past what happened that night in order for us to start something new.

I place my hand over hers, and before she can pull away, I tighten my fingers around hers. Her eyes dart to mine, and even though she's uncomfortable, she doesn't look away.

"I'm sorry, Doc. I shouldn't have left you that night."

Her lips part and the look in her eyes sharpen as if she's about to shut me down.

"Please let me say this," I whisper urgently.

I expect her to look away, or to tell me to go to hell, but instead, she nods.

I let out a sigh of relief. That's one win for me.

"I'm not going to apologize for making love to you."

Her eyes soften until they look bruised, and I hate that she's still hurting.

"Just before you got to my place, my mom had called Logan. I refuse to take any of her calls. She... let's just say she wasn't the best mother. Every time she calls..." I shake my head and take a deep breath to control the anger that's always threatening to rise to the surface when I think of *that* woman. "I can't think of her and not get angry."

Leigh's body relaxes into the chair.

Thank God. She's listening to me.

"I was drowning in anger when you got there. Then I saw how upset you were and fuck... I swear I could feel your pain. If we had just hate-fucked, I would definitely be on my knees right now, begging your forgiveness for making a shitty situation so much worse. But what happened between us that night – you were my first in so many ways."

She tilts her head and gives me a look which clearly says she thinks I'm talking shit.

"Willow told me about the screw crew list, Jaxson. I was definitely not your first."

I turn my body towards her and placing my left arm on the table, I lean closer to her. The sweet scent of her perfume makes me inhale deeper.

Fuck, I've missed the smell of her.

"You're the only woman I've kissed, Doc."

I let the information sink in and watch her lips part on a silent gasp.

"Why?" she whispers.

"You're different from any other woman I've ever met. With you, it felt right."

"You're also the only woman I've made love to. Every time I try with someone else, I see you. I've tried, and… I can't."

Hurt flickers in her eyes when she says, "You've tried?"

This part of the conversation sucks. Fuck, I wish I could just skip it.

"I've tried and failed quite a few times."

157

She lets out a shaky breath. "What does that have to do with me?"

My eyes trail over her face, taking in her soft skin and those eyes... fuck, *those eyes*. I can see my future in them.

"*Everything*. It has everything to do with you, and that's why I want to get to know you."

She shakes her head and looks down at our joined hands.

"It was just sex, Jaxson."

I take hold of her chin and lift her face back to mine.

"You're not a liar, Doc. We both know it wasn't just sex."

When she doesn't admit it, I let go of her chin and move my hand to her neck. I brush my fingers over her sensitive skin and watch as goosebumps appear.

I wait her out as she reacts to my touch. I need to hear it from her.

"It's nothing but a physical reaction. It doesn't mean anything," she argues.

I lean into her and press my mouth to her ear. "What about the fluttering in your stomach?"

She quickly places a hand over her middle as if she can hide it from me.

"What about that flicker of hope you feel when you look at me? Are you really going to sit here and pretend you don't feel anything for me?"

"All I feel is fear," she spits out. I pull back as the shock from what she just said, ripples over me.

"Why? I know I shouldn't have walked away, but at that moment, I thought I was doing the right thing. I'd never hurt you intentionally, Doc."

She stares at the glass of wine and says, "When I lost my mom, it hurt. I've never felt pain like that before. I couldn't rationalize it. When I was with you, you made the pain go away."

She brings her eyes to mine, and the pleading look in them makes me want to wrap my arms around her and never let go.

"For the first time in my life, you made me feel what it felt like to be loved by a man. Then you walked away. It felt like I lost you and my mother that night. It hurt…" she takes a trembling breath. "The pain was unbearable."

"Doc, I only walked away because it's what you wanted. The hardest thing I've ever done was walk away from you. You needed to hate someone, and I took the fall. But it's been six years. It happened in another life."

She looks anguished as her breathing speeds up.

"Another life," she whispers, and I can see it written all over her face. She knows I'm referring to what she said.

"I know a lot has happened between us, and I understand we'll need to take it slow. I won't rush you. I just need to know whether there is any possibility at all, that I can love you without you hating me."

I hold my breath as her eyes begin to shine with unshed tears.

Fuck, this is where she breaks my heart.

"I don't hate you, Jaxson. There was a time I didn't like you at all, but I never hated you."

"You used past tense. Does that mean you like me now?" I can't help but tease.

"I like you, Jaxson, but it doesn't mean we can be together. We hardly know each other. We're practically strangers, and I don't have time for a relationship."

"You don't have time, or you won't make time? There's a difference, Doc."

"I'm not relationship material, Jaxson. You need to find someone who will fit in your world."

"You are the only woman who fits in my world."

She lets out a frustrated breath and glares at me.

I'm not giving up. She can glare at me all she wants, but there's no way I'm letting her go, especially now that I know she likes me.

Chapter 18

Leigh

It's getting harder and harder to keep him at a distance. The same intimacy we shared the night we made love is enveloping us now.

Even the way he looks at me is the same as that night.

"Tell me what you're really afraid of, Doc?"

His voice is low and filled with so much emotion, it makes me want to cry. I can't lie to him, even if I wanted to. It feels like I've been hurled back to that night.

"I can't lose anyone else," I whisper. "If I let you in, I'll love you and when I lose you… I can't, Jaxson."

He frames my face with his hands and presses his forehead to mine. My heart clenches so painfully, I almost grab at my chest so I can try to ease it. He makes me feel so much that it's suffocating me.

"*When* you lose me? You've already decided I'll leave you. That's not like you, Doc. You're not the kind of person to assume things."

I stare at him with wide eyes. Everything he's saying right now is a reminder of why I fell in love with him.

He sees me. He understands me.

But he also has the power to hurt me in such a way that I'll never recover from it.

I turn my face away from him because if I look at him any longer, I'll give in to this pull between us.

"You saw me when I found out I lost my mother. You're the one person who saw what it did to me. It will be so much worse when I lose you. If I allow myself to love you, I'll love you with everything I am."

Please understand! It already hurts too much.

I close my eyes, as I whisper, "Jaxson, the pain will destroy me."

"Give me a chance to show you I won't leave you," he pleads. "I will never walk away from you willingly."

I smile sadly because that's just it. "You might not have a choice one day. We all die. If you were to die because I couldn't save you... I don't even know how to process the thought."

I can see he finally understands because he looks away from me, his face torn with emotion.

We sit in silence for a few minutes, each busy with our own thoughts.

When he looks at me again, he rests his right arm on the chair behind me. Being caged in by him doesn't help at all. It makes me want to lean into him because I'll know I'll be able to lose myself in him. I won't have to think about any of this then.

"Doc, when you lost your mom, did you regret knowing her? If you could go back in time, would you want to know her for those nineteen years and lose her, or not know her at all, and save yourself the pain?"

I gasp at his question, at once angry that he could even ask me something like that.

When I start to turn my face away from him, he places his left hand on my cheek to keep me in place.

"Just answer it. I'll let you get off this plane, and I won't bother you again if you answer it," he says urgently.

"Of course, I don't regret my mother. She was an amazing woman. I couldn't have asked for a better mother. I was lucky to have her for nineteen years. And yes, if I could go back, I wouldn't change anything."

"Why?" he asks.

I shake my head and glare at him. "You said if I answer it, you'll stop."

"Why wouldn't you change it, Doc? You could save yourself the pain."

"Because I love her!"

We're both breathing hard when the sharpness of my voice dies away.

I yank my face free from his hand and get out of the seat. I start to pace the aisle, needing to find some kind of release for this tension coiling inside of me.

Jaxson gets up and steps in front of me, stopping me from pacing.

"I'm scared out of my mind, Leigh."

That's the second time he's said my name. I'll never admit that I love it when he calls me Doc, but hearing him call me Leigh, makes my heart expand until it might burst.

"I'm scared of losing you. None of us have a fucking clue about what the future might hold. I could die first, or you could die first. We'd both be taking the same chance."

He closes his eyes, and he's so heartbreakingly beautiful, it feels like a physical blow.

"Mr. Hayes was the only father I have ever known. My dad bailed on me and Logan when we were too young to understand what was happening. My mom... she's out there somewhere because it was too much of a hassle to raise us. Mr. Hayes passed away soon after you left. I've lost every parental figure I've ever had in my life. I know what loss feels like and as much as it hurts, I'd rather have a day with you, than a lifetime without you."

I blink the tears away.

He steps into my personal space and brings his hands to either side of my neck. Tilting my face up, our eyes meet, and there's so much emotion loaded into this moment that I'm struggling to breathe.

"You would do it all again because you love your mom. Give me a chance to love you so you won't regret it. If our love is worth the pain of death, shouldn't we at least fight for it?"

My shoulders slump, and I press my face into his chest. I can't bring myself to say no again. I can't push him away again.

"I don't know how to date. I've never even been on one. I wouldn't know what to say or how to act. We live in different states. We can't fly up and down to see each other. We –"

He pulls me away from his chest and presses a finger to my lips.

"I will fly up and down. I will move heaven and earth to date you, Doc. Just say yes. Say you'll date me and leave the rest to me."

I swallow hard as my heart starts to thump in my chest as if I'm about to perform an aortic dissection.

"Yes," I whisper, already fearing that I made the wrong choice.

Shock flashes over Jaxson's face and then he leans down so that we're almost eye to eye.

"Really? Yes? You said yes?"

I let out a burst of laughter, and he scoops me up into a hug so tight, it lifts my feet from the floor. I wrap my arms around his neck, hugging him back, and it feels amazing to hold him again.

"Fuck, Doc," he says with excitement. "Thank you."

Finally, he lowers me down his body until my feet touch the floor. It looks like he's going to kiss me and it instantly makes me blush. I take a step back and straighten my shirt.

I might have kissed him already, but so much time has passed. I feel too nervous, right now. I'll mess it up. I just need a little time to get used to the idea of dating.

I glance shyly at him, hating the question as it leaves my mouth. "So we're dating now? It's done?"

The smile on his face gets so wide if he didn't have ears it would wrap right around his head.

"You're the most extraordinary person I know."

"You said that before," I mumble, not happy that he didn't answer me.

"You have such a brilliant mind, Doc. You can do things I'll never understand, but when it comes to everyday life, I have so much to show you." He closes the gap between us and wraps me up in another hug. He presses a kiss to the side of my head and whispers, "We're dating exclusively, which means you do not see any other men and I don't date other women. I'm going to be an asshole and claim you as my girlfriend."

I laugh when he says asshole, remembering that's what I used to call him when we first met.

"Okay," I whisper, too overwhelmed to say anything else.

"So does it mean you'll unblock my number on your phone?" he asks teasingly.

I laugh, remembering the conversation that led to his number being blocked in the first place.

"I'll think about it," I tease back, knowing I'll unblock it the second I step off the plane.

Chapter 19

Jax

Me: How was your day?

Doc: Exciting. I got to assist with a transplant.

Me: You're the only woman I know who gets turned on by cutting into someone's chest.

Doc: You still have time to back out of dating me. You never know what I might do in my sleep.

Me: Now you're giving me a reason to tie you to the bed.

Doc: You have a one-track mind.

Me: It lives in the gutter when it comes to you.

Doc: How was your day?

I laugh when the message comes through. She still gets embarrassed whenever I start to make sexual advances.

Me: Long and hard. The same as my cock whenever I think of you.

Doc: Do you talk like that to every woman you try to impress? (I say try because I can't imagine it working in your favor.)

Me: Nope, I only get dirty with you. (Admit it. It makes you smile.)

Doc: No.

Doc: Maybe.

Doc: Okay, fine. It makes me smile.

I let out another bark of laughter. Fuck, I've missed her.

Me: Send me a photo.

I wait for the photo to load and the second it's clear I frown.

Me: Who the fuck is the guy hanging on you?

Doc: Sebastian. I'm having dinner with him tonight, which means I have to go now or I'll never be ready in time.

She's having dinner with another guy? What the fuck? Anger flares through me like a wildfire intent on destroying everything in its path.

Me: You're not having dinner with him.

Doc: Why not?

Me: He has a cock.

Doc: So?

Take a deep breath, Jax. I press dial and wait for her to answer.

"I have to get ready, Jaxson."

I can hear her moving around her room, and then the sound of water filling a bath fills my ears.

"Are you going to bathe now?"

"I am. I can't go out smelling like half the hospital got stuck in my hair."

I switch off the TV and walk to my room. Stripping out of my shirt, I say, "Put your phone on speaker when you get in the bath."

"I can't talk to you and wash my hair."

"Doc, just put your phone on speaker."

I hear her sigh, but she listens to me. I walk into the bathroom and open the faucets so the bath can fill. I step out of my pants and boxers.

"Are you in the bath?" I ask as I put my phone on speaker, leaving it on the counter.

"I'm getting in. Just so you know, this is such a weird conversation to have with you."

"Are you in?" I ask again, as I shut off the faucets and step into the bath. I sink down in the water and hear her do the same.

"I'm in. Do I need your permission to bathe?" I hear the sarcastic undertone, which only makes me smile.

"Touch your breast." I intentionally lower my voice.

"What?" She sounds a little shocked.

"We're having phone sex, Doc. Touch your breast and tell me how it makes you feel."

"I'm not touching myself! Have you lost your mind?"

This time I can't keep my laughter back. I decide to go first, that way she might feel more comfortable.

"My hand is on my abs, but I'm imagining it's yours as I move it down my body. I want to feel your hand wrapping around my cock."

"Jaxson," she whispers. I can picture her cheeks turning pink, which is only more of a turn-on.

"Touch yourself, Doc. Place your hand on your stomach and move it down with mine."

"This will never work." I hear her mumble something vague. "There, happy now? My hand is on my stomach."

"Close your eyes and listen to my voice," I instruct as I shut my own eyes. "Move your hand down to your pussy. Imagine I'm there with you, Doc. I'm touching you."

She's quiet, and I can only hear the trickling of water.

"Where's my hand, Doc?"

"On my abdomen," she whispers.

"Slip my hand between your legs," I whisper while I fist myself. "Your hand is wrapped around my cock. It feels so good."

Her breath hitches, and it makes a groan rumble up my throat.

"Push a finger inside you and press your palm down on your clit." I start to pump my cock as I picture her flushed cheeks and parted lips. I can still see her tits clearly as they bounce every time I slam into her.

"Move your finger faster and press down harder on your clit."

"Jaxson," she breathes my name, and I wish I were there so it could really be my hand getting her off.

"That's right, Doc. Let me finger fuck you. I can't wait to feel you come again. I want to feel your muscles squeeze my cock. I want to feel your body tremble as I push you over the edge."

My hips thrust up as I lose my load and seconds later I hear her breaths hitch as she gasps. I can picture her clearly as she comes.

"You sound fucking hot, Doc. I really can't wait to be buried inside of you again."

She clears her throat, and I smile when she takes a few deep breaths.

"That was different," she whispers.

"Don't be embarrassed. Never be embarrassed with me."

"Okay."

A bell chimes and instantly my after sex bliss evaporates.

"Shit! I'm not ready." I hear water sloshing all over the place as she scrambles to get out of the bath.

"You're not going on a date, Doc. Don't make me fly out there so I can beat the shit out of him."

"I have to go, Jaxson. I'll call you when I get back from dinner."

"Leigh, don't you dare fucking hang up on me now." I get out of the bath and wrap a towel around my waist. "That's it. I'm coming there. You clearly do not understand what exclusive dating means."

"Shh... you're overreacting."

What. The. Fuck?

I hear her open the door, and then my eyebrows shoot past my hairline.

"Baby-girl, you're all wet. Scoot! Go dry your luscious ass while I mop up this mess."

God help me.

I rub a hand over my face as I cling to the last of my self-control.

"Don't you dare step in those puddles of water. I'll spank your ass fifty shades of red."

My vision goes spotty with anger when I hear Leigh say, "Jaxson, switch to facetime."

I switch to facetime as quickly as I can. Her smiling face fills the screen. A flicker of worry flashes over her face when she finally fucking notices how pissed off I am.

She turns the phone away from her, and on two guys and for a second time, my eyebrows hit my hairline.

"Jaxson, these are my friends, Sebastian and Ryan. Guys, this is my... Jaxson."

She didn't introduce me as her boyfriend.

"Hi," I say lamely, unable to think of something else while I stare at the one guy who's dressed in a blouse and heels.

"Oh my," he says, and I can't say I'm all that comfortable with the way he's looking at me. "You've been holding out on us, baby-girl. That's one mighty fine chunk of hunk you've managed to catch for yourself."

Then it hits. They're gay.

Thank fuck!

A breath rushes from me as relief courses through my body.

"He's a bit on the quiet side, but then again that might work in your favor. You know, with his mouth being busy down in your valley of pleasure."

I start to laugh, and I'm not sure if it's from the overwhelming relief I feel or the fact that the guy is hilarious.

"It's so nice to meet you. You have no idea how relieved I am you're friends with Leigh. I can't wait to meet you in person."

I mean every fucking word. My girl will be safe with them.

"Aww," the guy on the left swoons. He actually swoons. Well, there's a first.

"I love him already. When are you coming to visit?" He screeches and grabs the other guy's hands before excitedly looking back at us. "Double date!"

I start to laugh again, and I just know we're going to become good friends.

Leigh brings the phone back to her smiling face.

"How was that for payback?"

I chuckle thinking she really had me going there.

"Wait until I'm there," I say as I bite my bottom lip.

Her lips part as her eyes zero in on my mouth.

That's good to know. My girl gets turned on when I bite my lip. I'll definitely remember that for later.

"I can't wait," she whispers.

"Enjoy your dinner, Doc. I'll talk to you tomorrow."

"Sweet dreams," she says.

"They will be wet dreams."

She shakes her head and letting out a chuckle, she ends the call.

I sit down on the bed and take a deep breath. I have to get back at her for the prank she just played on me. How the hell am I going to outsmart a genius?

Chapter 20

Leigh

Everything is ready for Marcus' arrival today. Dr. Magliato agreed to assist me with the surgery. It's just as a precaution.

I'm a little worried that Marcus's condition has deteriorated. Both Willow and Jaxson told me he's become weaker over the past week. I'll only be able to assess whether his body will be able to withstand the trauma of surgery once I see him.

I knock on Dr. Magliato's office door.

"Do you have a moment? I'd like to discuss Mr. Reed's surgery."

"I have a few minutes before I have to scrub in."

I sit down, and like always, I get right to the heart of the matter.

"If his condition has deteriorated, I would like to get him on the table as soon as we can."

She looks at her schedule, and I lean forward, trying to get a glimpse of it.

"The theater is booked until one am. If it's an emergency, then we'll have to perform the surgery at one."

That means I'll be working a twenty-two-hour shift. She sees the worry on my face. I need to be rested for Marcus' surgery.

"There's still time before he arrives. Go sleep for a few hours."

I let out a sigh of relief. "Thank you, Doctor."

As I walk out of her office, I thank my lucky stars the hospital is backing me on this. I stop by the nurses' station on my way to the on-call room.

"If you need me, I'll be in the on-call room," I say to Sebastian.

"That's a good idea. Go rest that pretty head of yours. I've got you covered."

I smile at him and then go get some much-needed sleep.

When I wake up, and my eyes land on the watch against the wall, and I realize I slept three hours. I dart up with a shock. Damn it! I only wanted to nap for an hour. I look for my phone to see why my alarm didn't

181

go off. When I can't find it, I get off the bed to look under it.

"Sebastian has your phone."

I swing around at the sound of Jaxson's voice.

"What are you doing here?" I ask, surprised.

Then a wave of happiness washes over me, and before I can compose myself, I run to him. My body slams into his, and I throw my arms around his neck. The second his arms wrap around me, I feel a sense of calm wash over me.

"What did I do to deserve this welcome?" he asks as he presses his face into my neck and takes a deep breath.

I pull a little back, feeling embarrassed that I just threw myself at him.

"I was surprised," I mumble, not ready to admit out loud I've missed him.

He smiles at me and presses a kiss to my forehead.

"Yeah, I missed you too, Doc."

I shake my head and smile, wondering when I'll learn that I can't hide anything from him. He sees right through me.

"I brought you a sandwich and coffee. I thought you could use it before you get back to work."

He has our late lunch set up at a small table in the corner. As I take a seat, I can't help but glance at him. He's dressed in a dark grey suit. Every time I see him, he looks more gorgeous.

I moan into my cup as I take a deep breath of the aroma.

Jaxson clears his throat, pulling me out of my caffeine-induced coma.

When our eyes meet, I still. There's so much heat sizzling in the look he's giving me that I feel an intense fluttering of desire. I try to hide it by taking a bite of my sandwich.

"Thank you for this. When you live on cafeteria food, this tastes like a five-star meal."

"You're welcome, Doc." We eat in comfortable silence, stealing smiles, and secret looks.

I constantly warn myself not to let things move too fast, but whenever I'm with Jaxson, time doesn't seem to matter.

When we're done eating, I quickly clear the table. Before we leave the lounge, Jaxson slips an arm around my waist. When he leans into me, my heart shoots off into a wild beat. He stops less than an inch from my mouth, and I feel a slither of frustration.

"Do you have plans for New Year's Eve?"

"Just work. My shift starts at seven pm."

"Will you spend the day with me?"

I nod and for the slightest moment, our lips touch. Jaxson grins as he pulls away. It's the first time I've seen him grin in years, and I'm not prepared for the impact of it. Then he bites his bottom lip, and I'm lost in a fog of lust.

Shit, that's hot.

When I notice the teasing look in his eyes, I slap his shoulder.

"You did that on purpose."

"Just a little payback for the heart attack you gave me the other night."

"Oh, so we're playing that game?" I smile mischievously.

He shrugs. "Give it your best shot, Doc."

I lean into him and raise myself on my toes until I get to his ear. Sending a breath of hot air over his skin, I drop my hand to his hip. As I brush my lips down the curve of his jaw, I move my hand down the front of his thigh, dangerously close to his cock.

I've never done something like this, but with Jaxson, it feels natural. I can't explain what it is

184

exactly, although I've spent many hours thinking about it.

When I feel his jaw clenching under my mouth, I pull back with a huge grin on my face.

"Thanks for lunch. I'll see you later." I slip out of the room and laugh as I hear him growl something about me being a cock tease.

Chapter 21

Jax

I follow Leigh out of the on-call room. When she leans over the counter at the nurses' station, I can't resist slapping her ass.

She gasps and looks at me with wide eyes, a blush creeping up her face. I wink at her, which only makes the blush deepen.

When we arrived at the hospital, I first made sure Marcus got settled in before I went in search of Leigh. If it weren't for Sebastian, I never would've found her. I never knew how satisfying it could be to watch someone sleep.

I press the button to call for an elevator and glance over my shoulder. I smile as I watch Leigh shrug on her white coat while talking to another doctor.

The elevator pings, and as the doors start to open, I step out of the way so the medical staff can exit.

A commotion behind me has me glancing back at the nurses' station. Sebastian's face turns red, and he's grabbing at his throat.

I run back to them as Leigh moves in behind Sebastian, wrapping her arms around him. She's so much smaller and not strong enough to give him the Heimlich. Suddenly a chewed-up pen cap shoots from his mouth and lands close to my feet.

Leigh rubs his back, checking to see if he's okay, while I stand with my mouth hanging open.

Guess I was wrong. My girl knows how to handle herself.

Tears spill from Sebastian's eyes, and it's clear he's upset from choking.

"You don't have to be so dramatic," a man snaps at Sebastian. "Get back to work."

"Dr. Langley," Leigh gasps, "That's unprofessional behavior."

The doctor glares at Leigh and takes a step towards her. He gives her a condescending look, which has my heart pumping with anger.

I step forward, positioning myself behind Leigh and next to Sebastian. I glare at the man, daring him to try anything.

"If Mr. Ward can't do his work, he shouldn't be here," the man sneers, clearly not recognizing danger when it's right in front of him.

I take hold of Leigh's shoulders and move her to the side, so I can step right up to the doctor.

It's clear this guy has a personal issue with Sebastian because he's gay.

"My friend just choked, and you're rude. You owe him an apology." The doctor frowns darkly at me, and I love the fact that he has to look up at me. "Your methods of intimidation don't quite have the same effect when the person you're facing is twice your size. How about that apology?" I growl, giving him a final look of warning that he's about to meet my fist.

He directs the glare at Sebastian. "I apologize," he bites the words out.

"Mr. Ward," I whisper darkly. "I apologize, Mr. Ward."

The doctor rambles the apology off and rushes away from us. Fuck, I hate bullies. If that had happened on my turf, they would've carried him away on a stretcher.

"My hero," Sebastian shrieks behind me and grabs me in a hug.

I'm stunned for a moment, but when he starts to cry, I hug him back. He hardly reaches my shoulder, and I can clearly see the weird looks from the other people standing around the nurses' station.

"You're okay, it's just shock," I say to comfort him.

My words make him cry harder, and I seriously don't give a flying fuck what the other people might think. My friend is upset, and there's no way in hell I won't comfort him.

Keeping my arm around him, I guide him down the hall and into the nearest waiting room. I spot tissues and grab a couple.

"Here you go," I whisper, surprised by how protective I feel of him.

He removes one arm from around me and takes it with a trembling hand. I stand with my arms wrapped around him, as he wipes the tears from his face.

I glance at Leigh, and the look on her face takes my breath away. It's a life-altering moment when you see the woman you love looking back at you with admiration.

When Sebastian calms down, he gives me another hug.

189

"Our baby-girl did good," he whispers hoarsely. "She saved my ass. Poor Ryan would've been devastated if I died. I mean, it's a really great ass."

Sebastian turns and shows me his ass which makes me laugh.

"Yeah, Ryan is a lucky man," I say between bouts of laughter.

"Thank you for taking care of Dr. Pussy-deprived," Sebastian says, returning to his normal sassy self.

I'm still recovering from laughing when the next fit hits. "Pussy-deprived?" I ask as I try to gasp for air.

"Yeah, it's actually sad. I think he's so grumpy because he doesn't get laid. Then again, he's so sour I bet his dick is all shriveled."

When I finally stop laughing, I take hold of his shoulder and pull him to my chest, while asking, "Do you feel better now?"

He hugs me back and nods against my chest.

"I do. My make-up is ruined, but it can be fixed."

He pulls back, and excitement makes his eyes shine.

"You know what this calls for?"

I shake my head.

"A double date," he shrieks while clapping his hands. "I'll call Ryan and tell him to get ready."

"I need to check on Marcus before you call him. If Marcus is stable, we can go out to dinner," Leigh says.

Sebastian pushes Leigh out the door. "What are you waiting for? Go, do your rounds."

When the door closes behind Leigh, Sebastian turns back to me. A tear rolls down his cheek, which makes me step closer.

Placing a hand on his shoulder, I ask, "You okay?"

He nods and looks up at me with such a sincere expression, it hits me right in the gut.

"Thank you, Jaxson."

"For what? I didn't do much."

"Dr. Langley makes it abundantly clear every chance he gets, that he's homophobic. You treated me like a human. To me, it makes all the difference in the world. People don't always understand what it's like to be a woman trapped in a man's body. They tend to judge me because I'm different."

I make a promise right here to never treat Sebastian and Ryan any different from the way I would treat the other women in my life.

I pull him to my chest and press a kiss to the top of his head. "It's because they don't bother to see the amazing person you are." I look down at him so he can see I mean what I say. "It doesn't matter what sex you are, Sebastian. You have a beautiful soul, babe. Don't let anyone tell you differently. Go fix your make-up while I check on Marcus."

Chapter 22

Leigh

Marcus looks better than I expected.

"I have your surgery scheduled for the twenty-ninth at five pm. Dr. Magliato will assist me. You'll be in good hands, Marcus," I say as I complete the chart.

"Thanks, Doc."

I smile at him. "You're welcome. Relax until then."

I walk out just as Jaxson is coming in. We meet in the doorway, and he presses a kiss to my forehead.

"Is he okay?" he whispers.

"Yes, he just needs to rest. Is Sebastian okay?"

Jaxson gives me a reassuring smile. "He is. I'll be here while you finish up."

"I'll come to get you." I squeeze his arm before returning to my rounds.

When I'm done, and I peek into Marcus' room, I smile widely. Jaxson is playing cards with him.

"Dude, just because you're sick doesn't mean I'll let you cheat. Take back that card."

"It slipped," Marcus grumbles.

"Hey, guys." I walk in, and it's only then that I realize Willow isn't here. "Where's Willow? I thought she was coming?"

"I don't want her here," Marcus snaps coldly.

"I'm taking my girl out to dinner. Try to get some sleep," Jaxson says as he gets up.

He takes hold of my arm and starts to pull me from the room.

"Night, Marcus," I say over my shoulder before the door shuts behind us.

"Sorry about that," I apologize. "I thought they were back together."

Jaxson links our hands and brings the back of my hand to his mouth. He presses a kiss to my skin.

"It's okay, Doc. I swear those two are giving me whiplash. I really thought they would last this time, but Marcus broke it off this morning."

"I need to phone her later to hear how she's handling it."

Jaxson presses the button for the elevator, and I lean into his side as we wait. It's nice to have him here. I

194

didn't think he would fit into my world, but after seeing him with Sebastian, it's clear I was worried for no reason.

"Sebastian went to pick up Ryan. They'll meet us at the restaurant."

We step into the elevator, and I turn my body into his. I place my hand on his jaw, wanting to feel the roughness of his bristles on my skin.

"Thank you for being such an incredible man and for comforting Sebastian. I know he can get quite emotional, but I love him."

"He's my friend too. Sebastian and I have something pretty remarkable in common."

"What? It's definitely not your sense of style. I can't imagine you wearing pink lipstick."

He lets out a burst of laughter before he whispers, "You. We have you." He turns his face into my hand and presses a kiss to my palm. "You're never getting rid of me."

"Oh yeah?" I tease as I curl my fingers into his shirt. "Not even when I start spouting facts?"

He shakes his head. "Not even when you throw equations at me."

His hands slip to my butt, and he grabs me tightly, lifting me up against his body. His mouth trails over my jaw until it reaches my ear.

"I need to get the dating out of the way, so we can get to the sex part of this relationship."

I can feel his hard length pressing into me, and it makes me groan.

"I can't wait either," I admit.

Chapter 23

Jax

When we get to the restaurant, Sebastian and Ryan are already waiting. As we near the table, Ryan gets out of his seat and hugs me.

He doesn't need to say anything, because the grateful look he gives me says it all.

After we've placed our order, I ask, "So how long have you been married?"

"We celebrated our fifth anniversary this past October. My delicious chunk of hunk can't get enough of me," Sebastian says, placing his hand over Ryan's.

"Oh, wow, congrats."

The waitress brings our drinks, and I lift my glass to the men across from me.

"Here's to another fifty years."

"I'll drink to that," Ryan says. He presses a tender kiss to Sebastian's mouth, and when I look at Leigh, it's to catch her smiling up at me.

"How did you and Leigh meet," Sebastian asks.

"She spilled soda all over herself and then called me an asshole."

"You were laughing at me," Leigh says, pretending to look offended.

"Yeah, I guess I deserved it."

Everyone laughs, and the conversation flows smoothly, the only interruption being when the waitress bringing our orders.

I learn that Sebastian and Ryan were best friends in school. They were both in love with each other, but neither had the guts to make the first move until they moved in together. Ryan liked to sleep in the nude, and when Sebastian brought him some coffee, it turned into an X-rated movie.

"I didn't go to the prom because I was hung up on this ass next to me," Sebastian says. "He took a date. I was jealous as hell and let me tell you, green is so not my color."

"Did you go to your prom?" Leigh asks me, and it reminds me she never attended school and had missed out on those experiences.

"No, I didn't. I think Logan was the only one… oh wait, that was for Mia's prom. None of us went to ours."

"Willow once told me you had tutors. At what age did you graduate from school?"

"Thirteen. I spent six years in Boston, and then I met you. You know the rest."

"What's your favorite memory of when you were a kid?" I need to hear her tell me something normal.

"Let me think." She takes a sip of her wine and smiles. "I was four. Mom gave me my very own first aid bag. It had a real stethoscope in it. That night I fell asleep listening to her heart beating. That's when I realized I wanted to learn everything I could about the heart."

I watch her eyes light up at the memory, and I make a promise to myself to do my best to keep that light shining inside of her.

"What's your favorite memory?" she asks, resting her chin on the palm of her hand.

"That's easy," I say, smiling as the memory flashes through my mind. "I had anger issues during my senior year. One day a kid pissed me off, and I punched him. So there I was, waiting to have my ass handed to me by the principal when Mr. Hayes walked in. He drove me to our local gym and took out a contract for me. He spent the entire afternoon punching a bag with me. He always had time for me. I can't remember him ever saying no to anything."

"I'm sorry you lost him," she whispers.

"I didn't lose him, Doc. He's everywhere I look. He's in every lesson he taught me. Whenever something bad happens, I hear his patient voice telling me what to do."

"Aww… you're going to make me cry, and it took me ten minutes to put on my mascara," Sebastian complains.

After our plates have just been cleared, we're slowly finishing our drinks. Anticipation starts to build in my chest when it's almost time to go home. I booked a room at the hotel, but I'm saying a silent prayer Leigh will invite me to stay over at her place. I want to spend every moment with her.

"It's time to go, my delicious chunk of hunk," Sebastian says to Ryan.

"You guys go. The night is on me," I say when Ryan reaches for his wallet.

"Thanks, babelicious," Sebastian says, and when he slides out of his chair, he comes over to kiss my cheek. "Take care of our girl," he whispers before he pulls away.

"Are you my chunk of hunk?" Leigh asks teasingly once they've left.

I slip my hand under the table and place it on her thigh. It's a pity she's wearing pants. Not taking my eyes away from hers, I move my hand up inch by inch until my fingers brush against the V between her legs.

I lean in and whisper seductively, "As long as you know this is mine." I tighten my hold over her pussy which makes her cheeks flush. "I'm planning on burying my cock deep in your pussy the second we get to your place."

"Then you better settle the bill, Mr. West."

Fuck me.

My hand shoots into the air, and I call our waitress. Leigh laughs as I hurry to settle the bill. When I've paid, I grab Leigh's hand and practically drag her out of the restaurant.

The drive to her place is pure torture. I'm sitting in the back of a cab with a hard-on. I don't even bother adjusting myself. The second he pulls up to Leigh's place, I toss the money on the passenger seat and drag Leigh out behind me.

Her laughter fills the air, and she yanks her hand free from mine. She walks slowly to her front door while trying to suppress her smile.

"Stop the teasing and open the door, Doc," I growl behind her.

"Maybe we should go for a walk?" she asks. Her eyes are sparkling in the moonlight, as she glances over her shoulder.

I close the distance between us and press my chest hard against her back. I slip an arm around her waist to keep her in place and grab her breast with my left hand. I squeeze her soft flesh until her back arches.

"Open the fucking door, or I swear I will take you right here."

I slip my right hand down her abdomen and over her pussy while my fingers find her nipple, pinching it as I lower my mouth to her neck. I start to suck on her sensitive skin, as I rub her pussy through her pants.

Satisfied, I watch as she unlocks the front door with a trembling hand. The second she has it open, I push her inside and kick it closed behind us. Bringing my arms around her, I grab the front of her shirt and yank it, letting buttons pop free as the material gives way. I throw the ripped shirt on the floor and unclasp her bra. When I have it off her, I turn her around and grabbing her ass, I lift her up against my body. She wraps her legs and arms around me, and we breathe heavily as I walk in the direction I think her room might be.

"Where is your room?" I growl as I sink my fingers deeper into her ass. I can feel the heat coming from her pussy on my fingertips, and it makes my cock strain painfully against my pants.

"End of the hall," she breathes.

When I reach the room, I grind the words out, "Switch on the light. I want to see you clearly."

She hits blindly at the wall, and on her second try, she hits the switch.

I spot the bed and walk over to it, not caring what her place looks like. I'll take a look once I've had my fill of her.

Dropping her on the bed, I reach for her pants and quickly unbutton it. I yank the zip down, and when it gets stuck, I grab hold of the waistband and yank it down her legs. I'm relieved when her panties move with the pants. It saves me time.

I throw the clothes to the side and sink down to my knees in front of her. Grabbing hold of her hips, I jerk her body to the edge of the bed. She tries to close her legs, but I take hold of her thighs and shove them open as I move my shoulders in the way. Without giving her any warning, I latch onto her pussy, and I suck hard.

"Jaxson!" she shrieks as her hips bow off the bed. Placing an arm over her abdomen, I force her back down on the mattress.

She grabs my hair as I suck again, but instead of pulling me away, she fists my hair and pushes me harder against her.

I'll take it easy on her later. Right now, I have six-years-worth of sexual frustration to fuck out of my system.

I lick and suck her clit until she's writhing on the bed.

I thrust a finger inside her and curl it, which is all it takes. Her body starts to tense, and I back off, letting the orgasm fade away.

She lets out a frustrated groan and glares at me as I unzip my pants and pull my cock free. I quickly roll on a condom.

Crawling over her, I slip my arm under her and then lift her to me as I move us further up the bed. I drop her and grabbing my cock, I position it at her entrance. I have no restraint left as I surge into her with one powerful stroke.

Her hands claw at the covers as her body arches, and I take advantage of the moment to suck her breast into my mouth. I wrap my arm around her, liking the position a lot. Grabbing a pillow, I shove it under her.

Pulling my hips back, I first bite down on her nipple before I drive my cock back into her tight pussy.

Fuck, this is what I've wanted all these years.

My thrusts grow harder and deeper, and I relish in the feel of her tight muscles squeezing me. Her moans and quick breaths are music to my ears.

When she starts to tremble beneath me, I move faster and lifting my head, I watch her come apart, and it makes my own orgasm burst through my body, giving me the satisfaction I've only been able to find with Leigh.

Chapter 24

Leigh

I can't move.

Feeling boneless, I wait for Jaxson to come back from the bathroom. He's still dressed. Once he grabbed hold of me outside the front door, there was no stopping us.

He comes out of the bathroom, and just like the first time we made love, he brings a warm cloth. I feel self-conscious as he sits down and starts to clean between my legs.

He tosses the cloth to the side and then begins to unbutton his shirt.

I lift myself on my elbows and watch as Jaxson undresses, and I get my first good look at his beautiful naked body.

Every muscle is carved perfectly under his tanned skin. My eyes widen when they drop to his hips.

"How did that fit in me?"

He grins as he crawls onto the bed.

"Let me refresh your memory, Doc."

There's no explosive need this time, and it feels familiar as Jaxson lowers his body over mine. His cock rests right by my opening, but he doesn't push himself inside me. Instead, he places an arm on either side of my head and stares deep into my eyes.

I remember Jaxson said I'm the only woman he's kissed. It hasn't escaped my attention that he hasn't kissed me again.

His eyes take in every inch of my face, and it's the same look he gave me the first night we made love.

"What's your favorite color?" he asks.

I smile up at him, surprised at his question.

"If I have to pick, then I'd have to say red."

"Why red?"

"It's the color of blood." I laugh at the expression on his face as he shakes his head. "What's your favorite color?"

"Pink."

He didn't even need to think about it.

"Why?"

He grins playfully, "It's the color of your pussy."

"Eww," I laugh as a blush creeps up my neck.

"It's also the color of your cheeks when you're embarrassed or turned-on." Jaxson's eyes are tender, never leaving mine, as he asks, "If you were stuck on an island which three things would you take with you?"

"Coffee." Hell, that one isn't even debatable. "My laptop, but it has to come with free Wi-Fi for life."

"Why your laptop?"

"I can study while I'm stuck there."

He lets out a burst of laughter, and I feel his body shuddering against mine. It's amazing being skin to skin with this man.

I bring my hands to his jaw and brush my fingertips over his stubble

"I'll bring you," I whisper.

"Why?"

"You give good orgasms."

He chuckles, but I can see he's satisfied with my answer.

Grinning up at him, I ask, "What would you take?"

"You, Marcus and food."

"I didn't think of food," I muse.

"That's okay, you can give me blowjobs."

I scrunch my nose at the idea. I've never given a guy a blowjob so I don't know what it would be like.

"That's an experiment for later," Jaxson whispers as he brushes some hair away from my forehead. "You feel so good beneath me."

I can't argue there. It feels incredible having him on top of me.

Emotion tightens his features, and his voice is low and hoarse as he says, "Thank you for giving us a chance."

He lowers his head slowly until his lips slightly touch mine. I close my eyes as the anticipation of the kiss washes over me. I feel his breath on my face, and then he finally kisses me. I open my mouth to him, and as he slips his tongue inside, he lets out a deep groan.

We pour everything into the kiss. Our past, our present, and our future. We kiss the pain away and make promises we'll never break.

When Jaxson pulls back, I keep my eyes closed, scared of what I'll see. The last time he kissed me, it meant goodbye, and I won't survive it a second time.

"Open your eyes, Doc."

I shake my head, an anxious feeling spreading through me.

I feel his body pull back, and I hold my breath as I try to prepare myself for the blow if he decides to leave.

But he doesn't leave.

He pushes his cock inside of me, so slowly my body starts to tremble.

"Look at me," he whispers once his pelvis is flush with mine.

I open my eyes slowly and tears well in my eyes when I don't see a goodbye.

I see love.

I see the confirmation of the promises Jaxson made when he kissed me.

He starts to move inside of me, not once breaking eye contact. I wrap my legs and arms around him, wishing we could stay like this forever.

He pushes one arm under me and grabbing hold of my butt, he starts to move faster. Our breaths mingle, and the sound of skin slapping on skin fills the room.

When the tightening starts to build in my abdomen, I dig my nails into his back. As the orgasm shudders through my body, he slams his mouth against mine, kissing me with so much passion, it makes my pleasure increase tenfold. His body jerks against mine as he groans into my mouth.

When the last of our orgasms fade away, he kisses me deeply. He only raises his body from mine, long after we've come down from our highs.

When Jaxson pulls out of me, I see the flash of worry.

"It's okay. I'm on the pill."

"I'm sorry. I shouldn't have forgotten."

I can't resist and slap his butt as he gets off the bed.

"Oh, is that how you want to play this game," Jaxson growls. He scoops me up, carrying me to the shower, and I let out a shriek as cold water rains down on me. He steps in under the spray, and soon the heat from his body chases the chill from mine.

Chapter 25

Jax

I've been trying to distract Marcus all day, but nothing is working anymore.

I've tried playing cards, chess, and even scrabble. I've put on a comedy on TV, but he would just stare off into space.

So, now we're both just sitting here watching the minutes tick by, and it fucking sucks. I keep looking at him, thinking of all the great times we've had together. I wish I could read his mind, so I would know what to say to make him feel better.

An hour before surgery, panic flashes over his face.

"Jax, promise you'll keep contact with Willow. Watch out for her. Make sure she doesn't marry some fucker who won't appreciate her. Promise me you'll make sure she's always taken care of."

His voice is filled with so much fear, it makes me move to the bed, so I can sit next to him. Placing my hands on either side of his head, I lean over him giving him no choice but to look at me.

"Don't fucking start with this shit. You are going to be fine. You have the best doctor, and she won't let you die. Don't give up. Not now."

"I'm so fucking scared. What if I don't wake up? What if I fucking die, Jax? What's after death?"

Marcus' breaths come faster until he begins to hyperventilate, making the monitors go crazy, which fills the room with noise. Before I can call for help, Sebastian rushes into the room. He presses a button, and the noise ceases. I stand up and get out of the way when he places an oxygen mask over Marcus' face.

I can only stand with my hand, covering my mouth as I watch my friend break down while he needs to be at his strongest.

"Come on, darling. Take a deep breath. Look at me." Sebastian breathes with Marcus, who's eyes are wide with fear.

Sebastian keeps soothing him and places Marcus' hand on his chest. "Breathe with me, baby. Deep in, there you go, let it out. Deep in, and let it out."

He patiently sits with Marcus until he's calmed down. All I can do is fight the tears that are threatening to fall.

"Keep breathing," Sebastian whispers. He takes Marcus' hand and holds it while he makes sure he's okay.

"There you go." Sebastian removes the oxygen and smiles at Marcus. "Don't get yourself so worked up. You're in good hands."

Sebastian starts to pull his hand free, and to my surprise, Marcus grabs hold of him.

"Don't leave. Stay and talk to me. Tell me anything. Just keep my mind busy, or I'll go insane."

Sebastian sits on the side of the bed and smiles teasingly.

"You sure you want to give me free reign over the subject?"

Marcus nods as he keeps taking deep breaths.

"Okay, don't say I didn't warn you. Let's see…" Sebastian's face lights up. "Oh yes, you're gonna love this one. So, there I was, hiding in the closet cause it wasn't socially acceptable to be gay. I mean, I was literally in the closet trying on my Mamma's heels. She had a leopard print pair I really liked. She opened the door, finding me with my leg in the air, trying to force her heels onto my bigass foot."

Sebastian begins to laugh, and it draws a smile from Marcus.

"Darling, let me tell you my mamma was pissed. Boy, I thought she was going to whoop my bedazzled ass. She hauled me out of the closet and picked up her heels, holding them to her chest."

A sentimental look softens his smile.

"She was angry because I was trying to get my feet into her four hundred dollar shoes. She wasn't angry because I was gay. Even though I had to take the trash out for a week, it's one of my favorite memories."

"Have you always known you were gay?" Marcus asks.

"Gay is just a label. I've always known I was different from other boys. I wanted to stay home and play with dolls while they played with their cars. I chose to stay home and bake with my mamma while my brothers went fishing with my dad. I'm lucky. My family never treated me differently. My oldest brother would beat up any kid who tried to bully me. When I was confused about my feelings for Ryan, my mamma

215

sat me down and told me a soul doesn't get to pick its mate. You're soulmates because you share a soul."

"Do you believe that?"

"I do, with all my heart. I can't imagine my life without Ryan."

"When your mom talked to you about soulmates, was that when you knew Ryan was the one?"

"No, she just gave me a talking to so I would pull my head out of my ass and go claim my man. When I saw Ryan for the first time, I knew. I knew he was the right one because I kept going back to him. I couldn't let go of him no matter how I tried to fool myself. Trying to stay apart is like trying to tear a soul in half."

The door to the room opens, and Leigh comes in followed by another doctor.

"Are you ready to get those fragments out?" she asks Marcus while smiling warmly.

Sebastian gets up but doesn't let go of Marcus' hand.

"Can he come with?" Marcus asks. "He's a nurse. Is it allowed?" The panic and fear rush back into Marcus' eyes, and I wish I could be the one to hold his hand.

"You don't have to ask. I'll be there with you through the whole procedure," Sebastian assures him.

"It's time to go, Marcus. Would you like a moment alone with Jaxson?" Leigh asks.

"Please," he whispers, his voice thick with tears.

Sebastian kisses the back of Marcus' hand. "I'm right outside the door. Call when you're ready."

When everyone has cleared the room, I turn back to Marcus.

"You are going to be fine." It's all I can say. I need him to believe it too.

"Don't tell the guys about this. I don't want them to remember me being scared."

"Fuck, Marcus," I hiss. I lean over him and cradle his face in my hands. "You will not die. I will follow you right through those fucking pearly gates and drag your ass back so I can kill you myself. You're my fucking soulmate. Don't you even dare think about leaving me."

"I'm scared, Jax." He gasps for air as tears roll into my hands. "I'm so fucking scared."

"I love you." I press my forehead to his, and I can't keep the tears back any longer. "I love you. I fucking love you, Marcus Reed. You hear me?" I stare deep into his eyes as he nods. "I love you, and you will pull through this. Do it for me. I'm too fucking selfish to

217

lose you. I can't live a life where you're not in it. You're in my fucking bones. Promise me you'll fight. Fight for me."

He grabs hold of my wrist, and with a shuddering breath, he whispers the words I need to hear.

"I promise, Jax. I'll fight. I'll fight because I want to be there for every minute of your life. I'll fight with everything I have."

He swallows hard, and his face crumbles under the emotion, which only makes my own tears fall faster.

"But if I don't make it, don't think it's because I gave up. Don't blame yourself, because I know you will. Don't blame me for not fighting harder."

"What the fuck do I do if you don't make it?" I groan as the pain rips through me.

"You live," he whispers. "You fucking live for both of us. You live knowing I loved you... so fucking much."

We both cry because no matter how good Leigh is, there's a chance he won't make it.

Chapter 26

LEIGH

As Dr. Yang administers the anesthetics, Sebastian holds Marcus' hand. He presses a kiss to Marcus' forehead and smiles warmly at him.

"I'll be right here when you open those gorgeous eyes again," he whispers as Marcus starts to go under.

Taking the scalpel, I look down at his chest.

This isn't Marcus.

This is a patient.

He's a patient.

I take a deep breath and make the skin incision, and cut through the layers of soft tissue. I open the sternum with a saw and cauterize arterial bleeding points on the underside of the sternum to minimize blood loss. We use sternal retractors to maximize exposure, and the second I see the beating heart, I take a deep breath and allow my mind to take over.

Chapter 27

JAXSON

I sit in the waiting room, and I'm about to start chewing my nails when Ryan walks in.

"Sebastian called and said you might need some company." He hands me a cup of coffee and sits down next to me.

"Thanks. I just wish I knew how it was going."

"I don't know much, but I'm sure he's going to be okay."

"I hope so," I whisper.

My phone rings and when I see Carter's name flashing on the screen, I answer.

"Hey."

"How are you holding up?"

"I don't know. I keep going from hopeful to scared out of my fucking mind."

"We're just about to land. We'll be there soon."

"Hurry," I squeeze the word out.

Ending the call, my shoulders slump. I need my friends here.

The two people who mean the most to me in the world are in that operating room, and I'm scared that only one will walk out of there.

Ryan places a hand on my back, and that's all it takes for me to start crying. The worry is too intense. I can't breathe past it.

Chapter 28

Jax

Having Ryan sit with me helps a hell of a lot. Ryan's married to Sebastian, and knowing Sebastian is holding Marcus' hand right this second, makes it feel like I'm there with them in some way.

"Why couldn't we see him before surgery?" Hearing Mia's voice makes my head snap up. Seconds later, the whole crew comes walking into the waiting room.

"It's what Marcus wanted. You'll see him when he's out of surgery," Logan patiently explains.

"Hey guys," I say to everyone in general.

"How is he?" Rhett asks.

"Is there any news?" Carter asks a second later.

Ryan holds up a hand to stop any further question.

"We're still waiting. It's too soon for any news." He reaches a hand out to Carter. "Ryan Ward. I'm Sebastian's husband."

"Carter Hayes. Sorry, but who's Sebastian?" he asks, as he shakes Ryan's hand.

"He's a nurse here. He's currently with Marcus. He'll let us know the second they have an update."

"Thank you," Carter says, as he takes a seat next to Ryan.

Mia sits down next to me and gives me a hug.

"How are you doing?" she whispers.

I shake my head and let out a heavy breath.

Wrapping her arm around my waist, she rests her cheek against my arm.

I'm surprised when Della and Danny walk into the waiting room. I didn't know they were coming.

Danny smiles as she walks straight to me. She wiggles her way onto my lap and gives me a big sloppy kiss.

"Why do you look so sad, Uncle Jax?"

I drop my eyes from hers and whisper, "My heart is just a little broken."

She places her hand over my heart, as her bottom lip starts to tremble.

"Don't cry, Uncle Jax," she whispers.

I try to blink the tears away and suck in a deep breath of air, but then Danny scrambles to her knees, and she wraps her tiny arms around my neck.

"It's okay," she whispers patting my back with her tiny hand. When she caresses my hair, I lose it.

"It's okay," she keeps whispering as she comforts me. "Just don't get snot on me, okay? I'll ask Mommy for a tissue if you need one."

I laugh and cry at the same time at her words, and I have to admit, I feel a little better.

When I manage to control my emotions, Danny pulls back. She takes hold of her shirt and tries to see if I got snot on her. Della hands her a tissue, and she gets busy wiping the tears from my face.

"You're lucky, Uncle Jax. You don't have snot. When I cry, my snot runs all over the place. It just keeps coming and coming and coming." When she's done, she smiles brightly. "There, now you're all better."

"Yeah, Princess," I say as I press a kiss to the top of her head. "You fixed my heart."

After a few minutes, Danny crawls off my lap and gets onto Carter's. It doesn't take her long to fall asleep in his arms.

The room is quiet as we all sit and wait. Every time I look at my watch, only ten seconds have passed.

Suddenly the door opens, and Sebastian comes in. He freezes, while his widening eyes scan the room.

"Oh my, there's so much testosterone in this room my poor ovaries are going to combust."

"You don't have ovaries," Ryan says as he gets up.

"My imaginary ones. I think we should swap places. I'll comfort the hunks, and you go hold Marcus' hand."

"Sebastian," I say, ready to have a nervous breakdown. "How is he?"

"Oh, yes!" He finally remembers why he came here. "Marcus is doing well. I have to get back. Too-de-loo." He wiggles his fingers in a wave and disappears out the door.

"What the hell just happened?" Rhett asks with his eyes still on the door.

"My husband is a scatter-brain. All that matters is Marcus is doing well," Ryan says, sitting back down.

He places a hand on my back and locks eyes with me.

"Marcus is doing well, Jaxson."

"He is," I whisper as it sinks in. "Thank God."

"Is he allowed to wear lipstick to work?" Rhett asks.

I shake my head. I know it's coming from a good place, but Ryan might not think so.

"Sure. It's the same as any other female wearing lipstick to work."

Rhett nods. "True, I didn't think of it that way."

I can see another question coming, and I let out a groan.

"How do you kiss?"

"Fuck, Rhett," I groan, dropping my face into my hands.

"No, I don't it mean like that. It's just whenever I have to kiss a woman, and she's wearing lipstick, I end up with most of it smeared over my face. None of your women wear lipstick so I thought I'd ask Ryan."

Ryan chuckles, and I'm just thankful he's amused with Rhett.

"That's why you take them to dinner. If they eat first, you won't have a lipstick problem."

Rhett opens his mouth, but Ryan holds up a finger to stop him. He leans over me and whispers to Rhett.

"If you want to skip dinner, just let them blow you. It gets rid of the lipstick, and you score."

Ryan quickly glances back at Danny to make sure she's still sleeping.

Rhett looks impressed with the answer where he's thinking about it. "Yeah, I like option number two better."

"Eww... I'm right here," Mia hisses. "Ugh, I'm traumatized for life."

Logan starts to laugh but instantly tries to swallow it when Mia glares at him.

Trying to keep in her laughter, Della stares up at the ceiling while her face turns red from all the effort it takes.

Carter lowers his head, and his whole body begins to shake Danny as he silently laughs.

The next second we all burst out laughing and it helps to relieve a lot of the tension.

I give Ryan a thankful smile.

Chapter 29

Leigh

Every time I walk down this hall, my stomach knots.

I take a deep breath as I fight the tears. Normally, I wouldn't be affected by something like this, but because it's Marcus, I can't help but feel.

He was high-risk, just like Mom.

When I get to the door, I close my eyes as I try to control my emotions.

I need to be professional. I'm a doctor. I can't cry.

I feel a hand on my shoulder, and when I glance behind me, I see Dr. Magliato. "Would you like me to speak to the family?"

As the first tear rolls down my cheek, I nod. There's no way I'll be able to stop crying once I see Jaxson.

"Please," I whisper as I step to the side so she can go in first.

When she opens the door, I follow her into the waiting room.

Everyone is here. Jaxson is the first to stand, and his eyes find mine. My tears come faster, and I cover my mouth.

The blood drains from his face, and I want to tell him it's okay, but I can't get any words out.

"Mr. Reed's surgery was a success. There was a minor complication, which Dr. Baxter handled with great care. The patient is in recovery right now. I suggest you all go home and get some rest. You'll be able to see him tomorrow."

"Thank you, Doctor," Carter says with great relief as he shakes her hand.

Knowing they need this moment to celebrate that Marcus survived the surgery, I leave the room and rush to the elevators. When the doors open, I quickly step inside and repeatedly press the button for the doors to close. I watch as Jaxson walks into the hallway and our eyes meet for a split-second before the doors shut.

The cab driver keeps giving me looks filled with pity as he drives to the address I gave him. When he stops outside the house, I pay him.

Rushing up the stairs to the front door, I bang my fist on the wood until he opens.

"I could've saved her," I cry. "Why didn't you save her?"

"Come inside, Sweetheart," Dad whispers. He pulls me inside and shuts the door.

We walk to his study, where he takes a folder from his safe. He hands it to me with an unsteady hand.

When I open it and see that it's Mom's file, I drop to the floor and scatter the pages over the carpet so I can see every single detail.

I wipe the tears from my face with the back of my hand as I take in all the information, but when I get to the last piece of paper, I double over and cry into it.

"She had a DNR. It was her choice, Leigh. When her heart stopped, I couldn't go against her wishes."

I crumble the DNR to my chest and stumble to my feet.

I nod at Dad and whisper, "I understand."

When I walk to the front door, Dad calls after me, "Where are you going?"

"Mom," I whisper as I leave the house.

My feet automatically move, placing one step in front of another. The streets are quiet. Normally, I love this time of night. But not tonight.

When I get to the cemetery, I walk down the narrow path leading to Mom's grave. I stop in front of her headstone and hold the DNR out to her.

"Why?" I gasp. "Why would you sign something like this? You had no right. You were a mother. You were my mother."

I kneel on her grave and wait inconsolably for an answer.

"You chose to leave me," I whisper.

I lie down and curl myself into a small ball while cries rip from me because Mom wouldn't fight for me the same way Marcus fought for Jaxson.

I don't know how long I lie on her grave.

I lose count of the number of times I ask why.

I can't understand why Mom would choose to leave me.

I don't hear the footsteps coming up the path. I don't fight when arms slip under me, and I'm lifted to a chest.

I just hold on to the DNR – the proof my mother chose not to fight for me.

"Is she okay?" I hear Sebastian whisper.

"Yeah. Let's get her home," Jaxson says, and his voice rumbles against my ear.

"I'm all for leaving this place. Being in a cemetery at midnight messes with my mojo. I swear to you Jaxson, if I see a ghost, I'm leaving you right here. I'm too good-looking to become a zombie."

"You can't become a zombie," I whisper.

"See, I told you it would work. She can't resist setting me straight."

"Unless you're infected by the cat parasite, *Toxoplasma Gondii,*" I say, returning to my safe haven of facts.

"Say what?" Sebastian shrieks. "Woman, don't say things like that until I'm out of this place. OMG, I need to smudge my ass before I lose my bedazzledness."

I block out Sebastian's rambling and turn my face into Jaxson's chest, and I begin to process the facts, one after the other.

In medical school, most of the students had a DNR. A survey in our class showed eighty percent wanted less aggressive end-of-life care.

What they all chose back then didn't bother me back then, but now that I've lost Mom because of a DNR, I wonder what they knew that I didn't.

Chapter 30

Jax

I place Leigh gently on the bed and remove our shoes before I lie down next to her.

My heart breaks when I look into her eyes. I'm not sure what happened. Her dad called Sebastian and told him Leigh left his place in a state. If he didn't tell us where to find her, she would still be lying on her mother's grave.

I reach for the piece of crumpled paper in her hands and pull it slowly from her fingers.

I open it and when I see it's a do not resuscitate order, it all makes sense.

"When I closed up Marcus, I realized I could've saved her. Knowing that..." She curls into a small bundle against my chest.

I wrap my arms around her and hold her tightly, waiting for her to let it all out.

There's so much confusion and heartache in her voice as she whispers, "Why would she sign a DNR?"

I close my eyes, wondering if she'll ever heal from the loss of her mother.

"Dad showed me the file. He could've saved her. Her spine was also injured. She might have been paralyzed, but she would've been alive."

"Doc," I pull back, and placing my finger under her chin, I nudge her face up, so she'll look at me. "I didn't know your mom, but do you think she would've coped with being paralyzed? She didn't sign the DNR because she didn't love you. She signed it because she wanted to have a say in how she died."

"I wouldn't have cared if she were paralyzed."

"Put yourself in her shoes. We get married, and we have a little girl who looks just like you. She's fucking brilliant and has an amazing future ahead of her. What would you want for her?"

I can see she's starting to think about what I just said, so I continue.

"Your mom had a full life, Doc. Even if her spine wasn't damaged, it was still her choice to make. You chose to not sign a DNR for your own reasons. She had her reasons for signing one, and her reasons made sense to her."

"I just wish I knew her reasons," she whispers.

"Do they really matter? I know you have this need to understand everything in life, but Doc, that's not always possible. What matters is the time you had with her. What matters is that she loved you. You're so consumed with how she died, you're forgetting to remember how she lived."

Her eyes widen, and her lips part as the realization hits. "You're right," she breathes.

She sits up and looks at me with the same look of amazement she had the day I comforted Sebastian.

"Jaxson, you're right. I've been so selfish. I might not understand why she made the choice, but she understood. I've been trying so hard to figure out what happened that night, I've forgotten what she looks like."

She scrambles from the bed and yanks open the closet doors. She stands on her toes and takes a box from the top shelf.

When she places it on the bed, I sit up and watch her take the lid off. She climbs onto the mattress, and with a trembling hand, she reaches inside the box and takes a photo out.

A smile wavers around her mouth as she stares at it. I watch her look at every photo and then she pulls an envelope from the bottom of the box.

Opening it, her eyes dart over the words as she practically devours her mother's last words.

Leaning closer, I get a glimpse of the letter.

Leigh, I wish you knew how much I love you. You'll only understand how much when you hold your own child in your arms.

To the world you're brilliant, but to me, you'll always be my baby girl. I'm proud of everything you've accomplished, and I'm proud of the woman you will become. I know you will be successful in everything you do. I have so much faith in you, my baby.

If something happens and I have to leave, please forgive me. Please try to understand the world isn't always black or white. There are gray areas you can't see. There are things you can't argue, and there are things you can't justify with facts. If I had one wish for you, it would be that you could find a way to accept this.

Just because I'm gone, doesn't mean that I will stop loving you.

Always, Mom.

"Did you know gray isn't a color? It's a shade," she says, as she folds the letter and places it back in the box.

"I didn't."

"If you mix a color with white, it's called tinting, and if you mix a lighter color with black, it's called shading."

"Doc," I say to get her attention.

She opens her mouth to say something else, but I cover it with my hand. I pull her onto my lap and wrap my arms around her.

"She loved you. It's the only thing that matters."

She nods her head and glances up at me.

"You're so much smarter than me," she whispers, as a smile spreads across her face.

"Oh yeah? Hold on while I grab my phone. I want to record that. Fifty years from now, I can use it when you argue with me."

She chuckles while pulling me down on top of her. "Fifty years from now?" she whispers against my mouth.

"Yeah, if you're okay with that?"

She wiggles under me and pulls her phone out of her pocket. I watch her type something and then my phone beeps. I push myself up and dig my phone out of my pocket.

Doc: 1=0.99999999999999999999 ∞

"Okay, I'll bite. Enlighten me, Doc."

She looks at me with so much emotion I'm too scared to blink because I don't want to miss an instant of seeing the love in her gaze.

She leans against me and points at the screen.

"The equation represents the beginning of mathematics, which is us right now. The symbol represents the mysteries of infinity, which is us in fifty years."

I'm not sure what she's trying to say, except that she sees us together in fifty years.

"It means I love you now, Jaxson, and I'll love you infinitely for all the years to come."

The phone slides out of my hand as I stare at her.

"Say that again," I whisper.

"I love you, Jaxson. I love you so much it can't be measured. My love for you is infinite."

"How did I get so lucky?" I ask as I pull her against me.

"You got me wet."

I laugh as I press my mouth against hers.

"I like it when you're wet," I growl against her lips as I start to unbutton her shirt.

Chapter 31

Leigh

I'm busy with my rounds and checking on Marcus while Sebastian is giving him a sponge bath.

I hear a slap and tear my eyes away from the monitors to see what they're up to.

Marcus is covered from the waist down, and Sebastian keeps trying to push the material lower so he can wash Marcus.

"Stop it," Marcus growls as he pushes Sebastian's hand away again.

Sebastian shoves his hands into his sides and glares down at Marcus with a raised eyebrow.

"Darling, if you have a problem with me washing your ding-dong, I can always let Leigh do it."

Marcus opens his mouth and closes it again a few times, clearly at a loss for words.

"I don't mind," I say, just to tease Marcus.

"Hell no, woman! You want Jaxson to kill me? I just made it through one life-threatening event."

"What's it gonna be, babe? Are you gonna keep still or are you taking your chances with Jaxson not finding out you made his woman touch your ding-dong?"

"I can do it myself," Marcus wines.

Sebastian chuckles and holds the sponge out to him.

"Fine. Let's see you do it."

Marcus freezes, and after a few minutes, he glares at Sebastian.

"You want it to rot and fall off?" Sebastian adds.

"Fuck, you're worse than a woman," he snaps.

"Thank you, babe," Sebastian exclaims. "I'll take it as a compliment coming from you because you're being a real dick."

"Just fucking get it over with." He hisses while shutting his eyes.

I watch as Sebastian keeps it professional and quick, and moves on to wash Marcus' legs.

The door opens, and Rhett walks in.

"Hey, bro," he says, then he looks up, and he freezes. His eyebrows shoot into his hairline. "Dafuuug?"

I suck both my lips into my mouth to keep from cracking up.

"It's not what it looks like," Marcus defends while trying to move his leg out of Sebastian's reach.

"I've heard that one before," Sebastian mumbles.

Rhett tilts his head, and when it's clear he can't figure out what he's seeing, he points to the door.

"I'll… I'll come back later."

"Rhett," I cry as I start to laugh. I bend over and place my hands on my knees to keep myself up. "It's just a sponge bath."

Rhett's eyes grow huge. "You give those here?"

Sebastian rolls his eyes. "Not the kinky kind you're obviously well acquainted with. I swear, the postal address for that dirty mind of yours is smack bang in the middle of the gutter. Instead of standing there like a lost fart, come hold him down so I can finish. I still have other patients to take care of. Some of them happen to appreciate my sponge baths."

"Damn, woman," Rhett whispers as he carefully moves closer to the bed. "Is it that time of the month?"

"Don't you go and bring the bitch out in me," Sebastian warns while wiggling a finger in front of Rhett's face.

243

I bury my face in my hands and laugh until tears drip from my fingers.

I wish I could've recorded it.

When Sebastian is done, he gives Marcus a pointed look.

"Payback's a bitch, darling. As soon as your ass is mobile again, you have to sing karaoke with me. I won't take no for an answer. Keep that in mind next time you sass me."

When Marcus opens his mouth, I quickly cover it with my hand.

"It's going to be fun," I say.

As soon as Sebastian leaves the room, I look down at Marcus.

"Don't mess with his karaoke. He held your hand for over five hours. The least you can do is sing one song with him."

"I'm starting to wonder if I didn't die. I'm sure this is what hell is like," Marcus mutters.

Rhett sits down and props his feet on the side of the bed.

"If this is hell, I'm all for it. I can't wait to see you sing with Miss Sebastian. I'd pay good money for that."

Marcus glares at Rhett. "As soon as I'm out of here, I'm going to kick your ass."

Rhett wags his eyebrows. "You love my ass."

Staring at Rhett, I realize he's the male version of Sebastian.

Crap, I have to remember to never leave them alone together.

I move onto my next patient, and I can't help but feel sad. As soon as Marcus is better, they will all leave.

I'm not sure what will happen between Jaxson and me then.

Chapter 32

Jax

Now that Marcus is out of danger, Carter is heading back to New York. I've asked all the guys to meet me in Marcus' room.

Rhett walks in and pretends to look around for someone. "What? No sponge bath today?"

"Shut up," Marcus hisses, giving him a glare.

Rhett starts to chuckle, and it makes me ask. "What did I miss?"

"Nothing," Marcus says way too quickly, meaning there's definitely something I missed out on.

Rhett wags his eyebrows. "Miss Sebastian has been giving Marcus sponge baths."

"Fuck you, Rhett," Marcus grumbles, a smile tugging at the corner of his mouth.

Carter and Logan walk into the room, stopping me from making a comment.

"Thanks for meeting me here guys," I say as soon as they're all settled. "I want to discuss either opening a branch here or if you're prepared, to buy me out of IIP."

They all stare at me with confusion, and it has me explaining, "I'm going to stay here with Leigh."

Carter's face tightens with a have-you-lost-your-mind look. "Jax, in all the time we've known each other, have I not had your back?"

Now I'm confused. "What does that have to do with me staying here?"

"It's already done. Logan and I put in an offer to purchase a building, which we hope you'll like. Logan will stay here with you to help set up things and hire top management. I'm heading back today, but Rhett is staying for another week. Right, Rhett?"

Rhett glances away from the TV for a second. "Yeah, sure."

"You all fucking knew?" I let out a relieved chuckle, grumbling, "Assholes."

"If it's all you wanted to discuss, I'm going to go," Carter says. "I miss my girls."

Logan walks Carter out while Rhett's eyes are glued to the TV.

247

"So, it's the real thing?" Marcus asks. "You and Doc."

"Yeah. Are you okay with staying here?"

"Of course, he is. He loves Miss Sebastian way too much to leave her," Rhett mumbles.

"I swear to God, Rhett," Marcus growls, but then he begins to laugh, only to stop and wince with pain.

"Tomorrow is the big day," I say. "Are you ready?"

"Yeah, I can't wait to get out of here. Fuck, I'm dying for pizza, or a burger, or buffalo wings... shit, I'm going to stuff my face."

"I'll see you tomorrow morning." I glance at Rhett. "Don't make him laugh."

I leave the guys and walk up to the nurses' station.

"Hey, Miss Sebastian. Have you seen, Doc?"

Rhett called him Miss Sebastian yesterday, and it caught on.

I'm actually impressed with Rhett. He goes out of his way to treat Sebastian like a woman. I've even caught them flirting. I swear there's nothing on this planet that can catch Rhett off guard.

"Over there, lover boy." Sebastian tilts his head to where Leigh is coming out of an office.

"Thanks. Are we still on for Friday night?" I ask.

248

"Oh, hell yeah. I'll drag Marcus up on stage in a wheelchair if I have to. He owes me a song."

Fuck, I can't wait to see that. I chuckle as I walk to Leigh.

"Are you ready?" I ask.

"Yes."

I wrap my arm around her waist and press a hard kiss to her mouth.

"Let's go. I have something I want to show you."

We grab a cab, and when he drives to the address I give, I keep Doc busy by asking about her day. When the cab pulls up to the apartment block, I quickly pay and taking Doc's hand in mine, we climb out of the car.

Doc glances around while we walk into the foyer where the agent is meeting us.

"Mr. West, thank you for meeting with me."

"Jill, this is my girlfriend, Dr. Baxter."

They shake hands, and Doc gives me a questioning look.

"Shall we go up?" Jill asks.

We get into the elevator, and Jill swipes a keycard before pressing the number for the floor. When the doors open and we step out, Doc's eyes widen.

Walking into the living room, she breathes, "Wow."

I've arranged with Jill to give us privacy while I talk to Doc.

"Do you like it?"

Doc nods, her eyes darting all over the place. "It's stunning. I love the wide windows. Are you looking for a place while Marcus recovers?"

I take hold of her chin and bring her face back to me, and then I whisper, "I was hoping you'd move in with me."

I watch her closely as my words sink in. Her eyes widen, and a beautiful smile spreads across her face.

Her eyes begin to sparkle, and her chin trembles as she asks, "You want us to live together?"

"My love for you is infinite, Doc. When I look into your eyes, I see my future. You're my home, and if you don't like this place, we can keep looking. As long as I get to be with you, I don't care where we live."

She raises herself on her toes and framing my jaw, she kisses me softly.

"I love this place. When can we move in?"

I turn and walk back to the foyer. "Thanks, Jill. She said yes."

"Congrats." Jill walks over to us and hands us two keycards. "I hope you're both happy here."

As Jill leaves, Doc frowns. "That was quick."

"I already purchased it. I figured if you said no, Marcus could have it."

"So, it's ours?" she gasps.

"Yeah." I smile as I wrap my arm around her waist and pick her up against my body. "How about we christen it?"

I carry her over to the counter, separating the living room from the kitchen and set her down on it. I place my hands on the marble top and cage her in with my body.

"This feels familiar," she whispers as she leans back.

I unbutton the top two buttons of her blouse and drag the fabric over her head. Unsnapping her bra, I slide the straps down her arms.

Placing my hand flat over her breastbone, I slowly drag it down her body.

She falls back on the counter, and it gives me full access to pull her pants and panties off. When I have her naked in front of me, I position her legs over my shoulders and cover her breasts with my hands.

I trail kisses from her navel to her pussy, then take my time licking and sucking on her clit until she's a trembling mess from all the pleasure.

Chapter 33

Leigh

Walking into the bar, I spot the group where they're seated near the small stage.

I've been here a couple of times with Sebastian and Ryan.

Marcus and Rhett came together, and I'm glad to see neither of them chickened out. Sebastian is really looking forward to seeing them up on stage.

"Hey guys," I say as we reach the table. Jaxson pulls out my chair, and after I sit down, he presses a kiss to my hair.

When I first met him, I never would've thought he'd turn out to be such an amazing man. I might have had my doubts in the beginning, but they're all long gone now.

We order drinks while other people take their turns singing. Some are quite good, while others are clearly here to have a fun go at it.

I lean over to Sebastian. "You look pretty tonight. I love the pink streaks."

"Thanks, baby-girl." He blows me a kiss. "You look pretty hot yourself."

I give him a thankful smile for the compliment.

When we're on our second drink, Rhett helps Marcus to his feet, and we all watch as they make their way to the stage. Rhett grabs a chair for Marcus, and once he's seated, they both grab hold of a microphone.

I glance at Jaxson, who's sitting with a wide grin on his face.

Sebastian claps his hands excitedly as Marcus brings the mic to his mouth, and then he says, "We rewrote this song for Miss Sebastian. I didn't believe in angels until I met her."

He blows Sebastian a kiss, who pretends to catch it. The second the intro starts, Sebastian is overcome with emotion. I place my hand on his back when his eyes begin to shine. He brings his hand to his mouth as Marcus starts to sing.

"When we first met you, we couldn't look you in the eye. You're just like a queen, your beauty makes us shy."

Rhett steps forward and holds a hand out to Sebastian, who almost falls out of his chair in his hurry to get to the stage. After Rhett helps him onto the stage, he positions Sebastian between Marcus and himself.

He winks at Sebastian, and sings, "You're everything that's right in this beautiful world, but still you wish you were special. Well, we think you're special."

Marcus and Rhett look at Sebastian as they both sing, "When you feel like a creep, just remember we're the real weirdos. When you wonder what the hell you're doing here. Just remember you belong here."

Tears begin to spill over Sebastian's cheeks, and I can't stop my own from sneaking out. Jaxson wraps his arm around my shoulders and pulls me into his side.

Ryan's eyes never leave the stage, as the guys continue to sing to Sebastian.

"If anyone dares hurt you, don't worry we've got it under control. You have a perfect body. You have a perfect soul. Believe us, we notice whenever you're not around 'cause we think you're special. To us, you're so fucking special."

Rhett places an arm around Sebastian when he begins to sob, pulling him into his chest.

"Whatever makes you happy, we'll make sure you have it."

Marcus stands up and taking Sebastian's hand, he presses a kiss to it.

Rhett and Marcus close the song with the final lyrics, and I don't think there's a dry eye in the bar.

"You're so fucking special. To us, you are special. You're not a creep. You're not a weirdo. We love you, Miss Sebastian. You belong here. You're a part of us."

"Oh my God, you've totally ruined my makeup," Sebastian sobs into Rhett's chest.

Everyone breaks out in loud applause as the trio leaves the stage.

I wipe my cheeks, and when Sebastian sits down next to me, I give him a sideways hug.

"My eyes won't stop leaking," he groans, while he waves his hand in front of his face while taking deep breaths.

Ryan leans over to Sebastian and using a tissue, he wipes off the mascara streaks.

"I feel…" Sebastian looks at Marcus and Rhett. "Even though you made me ugly cry in public, you're both my chunks of hunks, and I love you madly."

We order another round of drinks, and when they arrive, Ryan raises his glass to make a toast.

"Here's to an amazing group of men, which of course includes me. To our beautiful women." He looks lovingly at Sebastian and me. "Here's to miracles and health, may we never run out of either."

We all toast to his words, and once Sebastian starts to dance, I lean back into Jaxson and watch as our friends have fun.

Epilogue

Jax

Eight months later...

I watch Logan set up the camera. It's become a hobby for him. He records every single get-together.

"Who's going first this year?" Rhett asks where he's sitting on the floor next to Danny.

We're celebrating Thanksgiving at our place.

"I'll go first." Marcus gets up and glances around the room. "A year ago, I thought my life was over. I don't know how to say this without sounding insane."

He laughs nervously and swallows hard.

"Just say it, babe. We're all a little nuts," Miss Sebastian encourages him.

"Yeah, we are." Marcus chuckles then his face turns serious. "It took me almost dying to realize what an asshole I was. It's still changing me every day. What I'm most grateful for this year are the fragments I had in my heart. If it weren't for them, Jax and Doc wouldn't have gotten together. I never would've met Miss Sebastian and Ryan. I've gained so much, being thankful doesn't even begin to describe how I feel."

"Thank God for permanent makeup," Miss Sebastian says as she wipes under her eyes.

She stands up and spreads her arms out to the room. "You're all my people. God, I'm so blessed." She looks at Rhett and Marcus. "My boys, I love you, madly. Thank you for encouraging me to have the surgery. Thank you for all the pampering afterward. Thank you for my B & V."

"What's a B & V?" Danny asks, looking up at Rhett.

I hide my face in Doc's neck, so they won't see me laughing.

"Your daddy will tell you later," Rhett answers quickly.

"Thanks," Carter says, not looking happy about Rhett throwing him under the bus.

Rhett and Marcus paid for Miss Sebastian's gender reassignment surgery. Miss Sebastian calls it her B & V, which stands for boobs and vajayjay.

Mia gets up and walks over to me. She hands me an envelope then smiles at Marcus.

"Is that what I think it is?" Marcus asks.

"Yeah."

I look down at the envelope, and the breath rushes from my lungs.

To Jax when he's expecting his first child.

It's Marcus' handwriting.

My hands begin to shake as I open the envelope and pull the page from it.

Jax,

I wish I could be there. Even though I'm not there physically, just close your eyes, because I'm right next to you in spirit.

I'll always be right next to you.

You're going to be an amazing father. I know this because you are an amazing friend. You have so much love and passion inside of you. You protect those you love fiercely.

You've got this.

Marcus.

I stand up and hug Marcus while taking deep breaths to keep from crying.

"Thank you," I whisper before I pull away. "I guess it makes it my turn."

I close my eyes and fight to control my emotions, which are already all over the place before I turn to Doc.

"I'm so thankful for you." I kneel in front of her and take her hands in mine. "I'm thankful for these hands. You gave me so much this year. You gave me Marcus. You're giving me a child. You gave me your love. You're my infinity, Doc. Please marry me."

I take the ring from my pocket and holding it in the palm of my hand, I offer her everything I am.

"Jaxson, it's perfect," she breathes as she takes the band from my palm, which is a simple woven infinity design.

"Yes." Although it's a whisper, I hear the word clearly.

I push the ring onto her finger and press my lips to it. Getting back up, I turn to Marcus.

"Seeing as you decided to stick around, will you be our child's godfather?"

"Are you sure you want to do that?" Rhett asks. "It's Marcus we're talking about."

"Rhett!" Miss Sebastian scolds him. "I will bend you over my knee, and it won't be kinky."

Marcus holds out his hand to me, and I take it without hesitation.

"I'd be honored," he whispers.

I sit back down and wrap my arm around Doc, pulling her into my side. I place my other hand on her very pregnant belly; then she covers mine with her left hand, and I stare at my ring on her finger.

Fuck, I'm a lucky asshole.

"My turn," Mia says, and we all watch as she tears an envelope open.

It's actually funny that Mia and Leigh fell pregnant at the same time. They've scheduled to be induced on the same day.

Glancing at Logan, I smile because our kids will practically be twins, just like us.

Mia and Logan read their letter from Marcus before Mia gets up to hug Marcus.

"I'm thankful for you, Marcus."

When it's Carter's turn, he places his arm around Della. "I'm thankful you married me." He looks down at his son in her arms. "Thank you for our children."

They named him Christopher Miles Hayes after Carter and Della's fathers.

Rhett gets up and tosses Danny in the air. She shrieks with laughter.

"I'm thankful for you, Danny."

When he brings her back down, she wraps her arms around his neck and presses a kiss to his cheek.

"I'm thankful for you, Uncle Ledge." She looks at him with serious eyes. "Will you be my fairy-godfather? I want one too."

Rhett glances at Carter, who says, "I think that's a great idea. We were going to wait until the christening but now's a good time, too. Danny asked you a question, Rhett."

Rhett looks at Danny with so much love as he says, "Princess, I'll be anything you want me to be. I'll be your fairy-godfather. I'll be your joker when you need to laugh. I'll be your knight when you need me to protect you. You own my heart."

"I just really want you to be my fairy-godfather," Danny says.

Leigh

Almost five weeks later…

"How could you do this to me!" I groan as another contraction hits.

Jaxson stares at me with wide eyes and a pale face. He's about to say something when Miss Sebastian intervenes from where she's sitting between my legs.

"He's sorry. He should've kept his ding-dong in his pants."

I begin to laugh, but another contraction wipes the smile right from my face.

"It's time, Dr. Baxter," Sebastian says. "You need to start pushing."

"I want painkillers," I cry. "Give me more painkillers. It's not working fast enough."

"It will kick in soon. Stop asking and start pushing. The sooner this little bundle of heaven sees the day of light, the sooner you'll feel better."

"You're right." I breathe through the pain and gripping Jaxson's hand tighter, I push as hard as I can.

I keep pushing until it feels like my insides are about to come out.

"Almost there baby-girl. One more push," Sebastian cries.

I close my eyes and push with everything I have.

"Oh, my God! She's beautiful. Look, we have a new baby girl."

Jaxson doesn't let go of me while Miss Sebastian clears our baby's nasal passage and the first shrill cry echoes through the room.

Miss Sebastian wraps her in a soft blanket and brings her over to us. She lays our daughter in my arms, and I lose all brain function.

There are no facts.

There are no equations.

There's only the miracle in my arms.

Mom was right. I understand now. Some things just can't be explained.

The love I have for Jaxson, can't be explained.

The love I feel for my daughter is so powerful, it crosses all boundaries. It covers all time, all space, every particle of my being. My mind will never comprehend what my heart feels for my daughter.

"We have a daughter," I whisper to Jaxson.

He pushes his finger into her tiny fist, and she instantly tightens her hold on him.

"What's her name?" Sebastian asks.

"Dash," Jaxson whispers. "Dash Marcelle West."

"Hi, Dash," I whisper as I look into her eyes. "Your name means infinity like our love for you. Marcelle means brave like your uncle, Marcus."

I send up a silent prayer to my mom, praying Dash will know only infinite love all her life. I pray she'll have her uncle's strength and her father's unwavering loyalty.

The End

Enemies To Lovers

Heartless

Novel #1

Carter Hayes & Della Truman

Reckless

Novel #2

Logan West & Mia Daniels

Careless

Novel #3

Jaxson West & Leigh Baxter

Ruthless

Novel #4

Marcus Reed & Willow Brooks

Shameless

Novel #5

Rhett Daniels & Evie Cole

Trinity Academy

Connect with me

Newsletter

FaceBook

Amazon

GoodReads

BookBub

Instagram

Twitter

Website

About the author

Michelle Heard is a Bestselling Romance Author who loves creating stories her readers can get lost in. She loves an alpha hero who is not afraid to fight for his woman.

Want to be up to date with what's happening in Michelle's world? Sign up to receive the latest news on her alpha hero releases →
NEWSLETTER

If you enjoyed this book or any book, please consider leaving a review. It's appreciated by authors.

Acknowledgments

Sheldon, you hold my heart in your hands. Thank you for being the best son a mother can ask for.

To my beta readers, Morgan, Kelly, Kristine, Laura, and Leeann - thank you for being the godparents of my paperbaby.

A special thank you to every blogger and reader that took the time to take part in the cover reveal and release day.

Love ya all tons ;)

Printed in Great Britain
by Amazon